NEW CITY, NEW ME

NEW CITY, NEW ME

NAOMI HINES

Naomi Hines

Contents

1 CHAPTER 1   1

2 CHAPTER 2   7

3 CHAPTER 3   13

4 CHAPTER 4   17

5 CHAPTER 5   23

6 CHAPTER 6   31

7 CHAPTER 7   39

8 CHAPTER 8   43

9 CHAPTER 9   48

10 CHAPTER 10   59

11 CHAPTER 11   68

12 CHAPTER 12   76

13 CHAPTER 13   85

14 CHAPTER 14   94

15 CHAPTER 15   100

16 CHAPTER 16   107

17 CHAPTER 17   113

18 CHAPTER 18   124

19 CHAPTER 19   133

20 CHAPTER 20   142

21 CHAPTER 21   153

22 CHAPTER 22   165

23 CHAPTER 23   174

24 CHAPTER 24   184

25 CHAPTER 25   195

26 CHAPTER 26   202

About The Author   213

I

CHAPTER 1

Whew, I knew pulling this mattress out of the box was going to be a pain but DAMN, I should have taken up that offer from the delivery guy even though he was staring at my chest and butt. I guess my natural DD works in my favor... sometimes. That is one thing guys like about my body. And oh yeah, I have a pretty face for plus size girl. I sighed and shook myself out of my thoughts and continue. I got the mattress into place finally and cut open the plastic and watched how the mattress expanded, hoping it was as comfortable as it said it was, as I needed a good night's sleep. Moving across the country was exhausting to say the least. Getting away from my past and starting at this new firm was the best thing for me. I needed to be a better me. I just wished I wasn't doing it at the beginning of summer.

After days of unpacking and feeling the need to go on vacation, it was the first day at my new firm, May & Jones Law Group. I was the attorney in the family law division. Dressed in my typical pants suit with my natural hair pinned up, I started to wear makeup but not too much. As I entered the office building, I met the young receptionist.

"Hello, my name is Kelly Turner, I'm the new attorney." The receptionist looked me up and down as if she pitied me, then looked at her screen. She then adopted a professional tone and smile and said, "Welcome. Follow me. She took me to the managing attorney of my department, Tiffany Jefferson, who also happened to be a black woman. She was confident, pretty and, of course, skinny. I had nothing but respect for her. I was introduced and she went over the normal first day things and took me to my office. Being in Dallas, I couldn't help but look out the window. So new and fresh no telling what will happen.

Tiffany introduced me to my fellow colleagues. There was Tim who looked like he was about to have a breakdown at any moment. Then there was Megan who looked like she clearly came from a privileged life. Lastly, there was Miguel. What you can say but.... damn! There just had to be one. His confident aura flowed from him with ease. He knew he was "FINE", and that was always the downfall — at least to me. Miguel had dimples, brown eyes and smooth light brown skin. Judging by the muscles bulging underneath his suit you could tell he worked out every day. When Tiffany introduced us, Miguel stuck out his hand with a smile. It was a firm shake.

"I hear you are from Chicago, is that right?"

"Yes," I smiled. "Born and raised." I wonder what else has been said about me?", I said with a chuckle.

"Oh, not much. Just that you are good at what you do."

"Well, now it is time for you to meet your legal assistant," Tiffany said. I nodded and looked back at Miguel while starting to walk away. He looked at me up and down with a smirk on his face.

I returned to my office where I found a professional-looking black woman already standing there. With a big smile on her face she said, "Hi, I'm Rochelle, your legal assistant."

"I will leave you guys to it and remember the meeting is at 11," Tiffany said.

As I discussed work items with Rochelle, she leaned over and said, "I'm happy to see another black woman here."

I laughed and replied, "I'm happy to not be the only black person here." After that, I knew we would get along.

Days later, as the weekend approached, Rochelle asked if I had any plans. When I told her, it was "just me and work", Rochelle looked disappointed and said, "Girl, get out and make some friends, it's more to life than work."

"I know, I know, Rochelle. I will look into getting some friends," I laughed. She was not wrong. As much as I missed my girls back in Chicago, I was no longer there. Back at home that evening I drew a bath. I was going to listen to music and try not to think for a little bit. But as I walked past my mirror, I could not help but see my stomach and rolls of flesh. Now that I was in my thirties, my stomach was no longer flat, and my muffin top had gotten a little bigger. And don't get me started on my flabby arms. Thirty-four wasn't so nice as I was heading towards a size 18. After the bath, I felt more relaxed and switched on my computer. My legal assistant's words were echoing in my head. I thought I would try some sites that organized gatherings for new people in town. I looked through some of them and decided on the wine and paint gathering. I realized that with my new salary I could afford more things now that student loans weren't making me so stressed. I clicked on a site that I knew I needed to go to but was dreading... the gym. I knew I would not be the skinny type but at least I could be healthy. New city, new job, and new me. I signed up for the pass and planned on starting with a trainer the following weekend. I did some work and watched some Netflix and went to sleep.

On Saturday morning, I went to the grocery store as I did not have anything in the apartment. There was only so much take out one could order. When I returned home, I did some work, then saw a familiar notification pop up. It was a message from my bestie Ariel. We talked for a bit realizing we getting old as we are reminiscing about all we use to do and realized I couldn't just go over to hers like I used to. It reminded me of what my younger days were like with her.

* * *

Chicago- Summer of 2000

I was spending the day at my best friend's house on the south side of Chicago where we both lived. Enjoying my summer before high school. Sitting on her steps, we gossiped about people we knew. Ariel, who I had known since I could remember, was my best friend. She was one of the sweetest girls, but you wouldn't want to cross her. She was the type of girl who always had my back. Also, she was also very pretty and physically developed for a girl of thirteen, but skinny. I was developed too but definitely not skinny — I had meat on my bones. The boys were crazy about Ariel, but I was always just 'the friend.'

As we walked to the bus stop to catch the 95th Street bus to Evergreen Plaza, a boy tried to talk to Ariel. Ariel brushed him off but, in true Chicago fashion, the boy kept trying the whole ride. It was a typically busy day at the mall, which was filled with all the pre-teens and teenagers who would hang out and there or at Ford City Mall on Cicero.

We walked into one of the entrances and started walking past stores. There was one store I wanted to pass by because of this one guy I had a huge crush on. His family attended the same church as mine and we went to the same elementary school, but he was a couple of grades ahead of me. He was tall, light-skinned and had the sexiest smile. He was also nice and confident. Whenever I saw him at the mall he would wave and I would wave back and smile, but I kept it moving because that's what we're supposed to do right? The guy is supposed to step up to you. Well, for me that never happened. Even when a guy talked to me it was to see if I could pass their number to Ariel. Even when there were a group of guys, I was just the friend to be nice to. Throughout elementary school I had crushes but being a predominantly white school, I was attracted to white boys, which proved to be a total failure as I did not exist in their eyes. The popular girls, especially the white skinny ones, pulled all the boys.

Even at the church functions, I remember when I was a teenager; people would tell one of my close friends (who was also skinny) how nice she looked but would never say that to me. This came from the women of the church. They would say, "Hey Ana, that dress looks cute on you." They would say hi to me and move on. I had five disadvantages: one, I was black; two, I was not skinny; three, I was an introvert; four, my religious upbringing. And lastly, I lacked confidence.

2

CHAPTER 2

My Father

Time to take it back to why I lacked the confidence to begin with.

I grew up in a religious home. That in itself made me different from the other kids. Also, when I started to gain weight around 5th grade, my father would straight up call me 'fat.' I could never do anything right in his eyes. An ex-military man who had turned to religion, he never knew how to hold anything back no matter how much it hurt. Critiquing was his fun.

I never once heard my father say I was pretty or smart, or anything positive. The only person who did was my brother, but he was not always around to boost me up, so it never stuck. My mother could only do so much. I guess you can say I had daddy issues. This went on all the way until he passed away when I was in my early twenties.

Black boys acknowledged my presence, at least, but that is as far as it went. But then one day that all changed.

Chicago Fall 2000

I started high school. I still had the weight on me, and I was a size 14/16. I was fully developed with a big chest and ass. It was an all-black and Hispanic school. Stepping inside my division room (also known as Home Room) for the first time made me realize real quick that the majority of people in my division were boys. I was my normal, nice, introverted self, and the guys acknowledged me. As the days and months went by, they talked to me more. One boy told me, "You going to be my baby mama."

"NO, I'M NOT!" I responded quickly. In my mind, it was just a joke. Years down the line, after high school, I found out out he had liked me for real but never pursued it as someone else came into the picture. That boy went on to become my first love.

Shawn

Shawn came my sophomore year of high school. By then, my curves were showing more, and it seemed my weight was going to the right places. Don't get it twisted, it still was showing in the wrong places too, but it was balancing. He sat next to me in division. I realized he was very attractive. He had LL Cool J lips and muscles. He spoke to me with a big grin that revealed his dimples. We talked and yes, the crush developed. To make it more interesting, his locker was next to mine. One day I was at my locker when I heard a guy whisper in my ear, "Hey sexy." I felt two fingers lightly pinch my butt. I looked up ready to punch whoever had touched me but saw that it was Shawn. All I could do was blush. This became a regular thing. Whenever I was at my locker, I purposely opened it up wide so it could hit him. (I know, I know... I was young!). Shawn would just chuckle and then walk past and pinch my butt again. One day his cousin, who I shared a locker with, blurted out, "Shawn likes you!"

Shawn quickly said, "No, I don't" and walked away. I never said anything. This is as far as it went until senior year. Graduation was approaching and everybody was signing each other yearbooks. I gave Shawn my yearbook and he included his phone number as a K.I.T (keep in touch). I didn't dial his number until the end of the summer. Even to this day, I remember what he said when he picked up: "I'm glad you called; I was going to change my number soon."

We started to date and fell in love. At the time I was still a virgin, and I consider him my first real boyfriend. I was starting college so I would go out more. The day came when I told him I was ready for the next step. I was nervous as he was the experienced one. I was also very self-conscious of my body, from the rolls and the extra meat on my thighs, to my muffin top, stretch marks and slightly protruding stomach. In Shawn's bedroom, he asked me if I still wanted to, and I said yes. I'll say he did not make me feel ugly. He kept telling me how beautiful I was with each stroke while caressing my whole body. Kissing me all over slowly. He made love to me. For the first real time, I felt fully exposed but pretty. It's a shame to admit but he helped unlock something inside me. He helped me see I was worthy of love and helped me start on my journey of building my confidence. Our relationship came to an end two years later because I grew up and he refused to. There were times we got back together in-between relationships, but eventually that ended as well. I even received a text randomly one day wanting to talk but at that point, I was officially done, so I blocked him. The last time we had another try I had told him that if we broke up that would be it. I guess he didn't believe me.

* * *

The rest of my Saturday day was uneventful. Sunday came, and I got ready for the paint and wine gathering. I tried to get cute with torn-up black jeggings and a cold-shoulder red top, gold dangling earrings, short heels and makeup. I was very nervous because as an introvert this was out of my element but I knew I needed to do this.

I arrived at the art event, which looked like a coffee shop by day. The hostess greeted me and directed me to the crowd waiting to be assigned to stations with easels. I walked and saw people of all races and nationalities, but there was no other black person. I had a slight panic. Did I make the right choice? There is always an internal battle that a black person goes through when they are the only black person in a group of people, especially white people. It's like we are not allowed to be ourselves and have to fight against every stereotype that society has created about us. It is mentally exhausting.

I looked back in the entrance and saw the first black person. I sighed with relief. I walked over to the side and looked over the crowd. I noticed some were going around introducing themselves to everyone. Some were looking and seeing if they could make eye contact with someone and then speak. This one woman made eye contact with me and started walking over. *OK, here we go.* She looked like a model. The perfect body and looks to match.

"Hi, my name is Lena. I just moved here from New York."

"Nice to meet you Lena, my name is Kelly. I'm from Chicago", I said.

"Ooh, I love Chicago! The food, the architecture; and the people are welcoming."

"Glad you liked it. The last time I was in New York, I think was 12 but I need to visit again.

"What brought you here?"

"I just joined an accounting firm, and the cost of living here is great. You?"

"I just joined a law firm and actually the same thing, the cost of living and the opportunity, along with just wanting to be somewhere different."

"I hear you on that. You seem like a cool person and not fake like some I've noticed. I don't need to be around a bunch of people to feel important."

OK, she might actually be someone I could hang with.

"Yeah, I noticed that too. I'm kind of an introvert, so I'm good at needing attention. Even though it goes against my sign apparently — based on what people tell me."

"What is your sign?"

"Leo"

"Oh yeah, you're an oxymoron. Haha!"

Lena and I took easels next to one another. We got along well; her family was originally from Lebanon. She actually did some modeling before. She loved R&B and was a really down-to-earth person. Guys were definitely trying to talk to her and she was turning them all down. To have that power was something I would never feel. Yes, I have turned down guys but this was different. It was as if she could enter a field full of flowers and pick whatever variety she wanted. I will never know what that feels like. We met one other cool person called Angela, from Atlanta. We exchanged numbers and decided to make plans for next weekend. All in all, it was a successful evening.

The work week came and went. Nothing really happened, except we received a huge case of involving a wife who was divorcing her millionaire husband for infidelity. Nothing unusual in that, except that this husband cheated on his wife with her *sister*. This was going to be interesting. At least I was billing a lot of hours. The only other unique thing was that I got partnered with Miguel. The cocky one. I found this out on Friday. At least I had the weekend before being subjected to Pretty Boy.

3

CHAPTER 3

"Where are you, Kelly?" Lena asked.

"I'm almost there; I'm in the Uber."

"OK, can't wait!" Angela popped up on the line and said, "Gurl! There are some fine men here!" I could not help but laugh.

"I'm pulling up now, I'll see you guys in a sec."

I climbed out of the Uber and saw a big line from the door of the Wild Boar lounge. Thankfully, I didn't have to stand in it as my name was on the list, thanks to Lena. Once I got in I texted Lena and was told they were in the VIP section. I made my way over and saw Lena and Angela sitting with drinks in hand, talking to a couple of guys. I sighed inwardly, envisaging the reality of how this night would go.

I reached Lena and Angela who both look beautiful. For a

brief moment, my mind returned to when I was younger, and I was the invisible one. Just the friend to be nice to. *Come on Kelly don't go back to that. New city, new job, and new me.* I put on a smile then,

"Hey Gurls! Finally made it."

"Hey Kelly!" said Lena and Angela. Give each one a hug.

"Oh my god, Kelly, you look hot in that outfit," Lena exclaimed.

Angela smiled. "I see you!"

"Please, look at you both! You guys are the sexy ones."

"Oh, my apologies, this is our friend Kelly. This is Mike and Charles," said Lena.

"Nice to meet you guys", I replied. They replied the same and went back to flirting with Lena and Angela. *Back to the awkward phase again. I need to get out of this.*

"I'm going to the restroom real quick. I will be right back," I said.

"We can come with? Angela and Lena agreed.

"No, I will be quick, I promise."

I checked myself in the restroom mirror and made sure the spandex was doing its job since I was in an off-shoulder purple Bodycon dress. I touched up my makeup and made sure the curlers I had put in my hair stayed in place. I was still amazed how much my hair had grown since I stopped using the 'creamy crack', also known as relaxer. My hair was now just past my chest. At the mirror I looked into my eyes and tried to give myself an internal pep talk. *OK, get yourself back out there. Nothing will happen by being in here.*

I was making my way back to VIP. They were playing old hits, and I bopped my way through the crowd. All of a sudden, I felt a hand on me. I turned and saw a guy who was clearly drunk or high grab my hand and say, "Come here, dance with me. You thick as hell." As I tried to pull my hand back he held on tighter. I told him to let go but he kept trying. My old south side of Chicago self was about to come and knock him out, but then another guy came up and said, "She said to let go, so I suggest you do so before I knock you out."

The drunk guy let go and said, "Alright, alright. She too thick for me anyway."

I rolled my eyes and then looked at the guy who had helped me. He was really handsome. He reminded me of the actor from the movie *Girls Trip,* the one Jada Pickett ended up hooking up with. I was distracted when he asked, "Are you ok?"

I snapped out of it and said, "Yes, thank you." I rubbed my hand and he noticed.

He stuck out his hand and asked for mine. I hesitated. Smiling, he said, "Don't worry I just want to check your hand." We went off to the side. He looked at it and massaged it for a second. I noticed the wire in his ear. I realized he must be one of the bouncers. He asked, "Better?"

I smiled and said, "Yes, thanks again. I better go, otherwise my girls will be looking for me." He smiled, and said, "OK, well enjoy the rest of your night." I returned his smile and made my way back to the VIP area.

Lena, Angela and I were dancing with some guys. I kept having this feeling I was being looked at. I looked around and saw the bouncer looking at me and smiling. I quickly looked away and blushed. *Nope, he could have been looking past me. Don't assume.* We continued dancing and drinking. By the time we left I was tired. I did not see the bouncer on my way out so I just left it at that. When I made it home I took off my makeup and barely got into my pajamas before passing out.

4

CHAPTER 4

I walked into my office on Monday with my iced coffee, Rochelle followed in.

"Soooo, how was your weekend gurl?" Rochelle asked.

"It was great. I and my friends went to Wild Boar. Great music and danced. Maybe too much haha. I'm still feeling pain in my knees and feet."

"At least you had fun."

"What did you do, Rochelle?"

"I spent the weekend with my man. It was our one-year anniversary."

"Nice! Also, congrats."

"Thanks, now I will go over everything for the day because you got a meeting soon."

"Ugh, Mondays"

We went over the day and was dreading my meeting with Miguel. I really don't like cocky men. We met in the conference room with our client and after the meeting, Miguel and I had our own meeting. We went over files and strategized.

"Tell me Kelly, what made you come here?"

"Well, I lived in Chicago all my life and I felt it was time for a change."

"So, you are running away from someone or something"

"I raised my eyebrow and gave him a look of disgust. "Well, aren't you making big assumptions when you don't even know me?"

"Hey, that's what we do in court, and I'm good at it."

I rolled my eyes. "Anyway Narcissus, we need to get back to this."

"Hey, at least I can walk away from a mirror."

"I'm shocked you even knew what I meant by that."

Miguel laughed. "Look who's making assumptions now."

"Ugh, I don't know how anyone can put up with you. I feel bad for anyone that dates you," I told him.

"Haha, they enjoy it." I shook my head.

"OK, moving on..."

At the end of the day, I finally left the office. I get home and realized I'd forgotten to go to the gym as planned. I put in my planner to start this weekend and no excuses. The rest of the week went by quickly and Saturday arrived. I got my lazy self up and went to the gym. I put on my sports leggings, which pushed everything in but were comfortable. I also had the bra that holds in big chests and put on a fitness top. When I got to the gym,

I requested a personal trainer. I knew I would need one. I was given a guy named Kyle. I had mixed feelings about getting a male trainer. One half of me knew I would be very self-conscious about everything I do; the other half knew it would help motivate me. The sales lady took me to my trainer and as we were walking, she yelled, "Hey Kyle!" A black guy turned around. I felt fear take over my chest as my heart started pumping fast. It was the bouncer. *How? How did this happen? Out of all the people in this city, it just had to be him.* I walked up pretending I was fine.

"Hey Kyle, this Kelly. She just signed up today and you will be her personal trainer."

"Nice to meet you Kelly", as he stuck his hand out for a shake and had a grin on his face saying I remember you.

"Nice to meet you too Kyle," I shook his hand.

"So, you are a bouncer and a fitness trainer? I guess they go hand and hand," I said.

"Yeah, it does. How is your hand?"

"It's good. Thanks for asking."

"Why don't we go over here and discuss your fitness plan."

I wanted to run out of there, but I knew I had to be open, even if I did not want to be.

"OK," I said and followed him. We discussed my weight goal and what the plan would be. I got to see my weight, which I dreaded the most. I felt embarrassed. Kyle had this professional tone and look the entire time. I could not tell what he was thinking and it was driving me nuts. I exercised for the next hour.

"Ok, that's it for today," he said.

"Thank god! I was feeling like my body was about to give up. And thanks." He chuckled.

"It will get easier the more you do it".

"Can it happen now?" Kyle laughed.

"No, if that was the case you would not need me."

"Umm, I guess you're right."

"I will see you here on Monday."

"OK, and have a good weekend. Hopefully, you're not working tonight?" I asked.

"Yeah, I'm working but I'm off on Sunday."

"Well, I hope you enjoy your Sunday."

When I made it home, I dwelled on how of all places and of all people this guy would be my trainer. I couldn't request a new trainer because what would he think of me? Ugh, I was stuck.

Sunday was a lazy day because my body told me so. It was stiff from the workout. Kyle would hear this. Monday came and I tried to pretend like I was not in pain as I walked into the firm, but Tiffany saw right through me.

"Are you ok?" she asked.

"Yeah, why?"

"You look like you in pain."

"Is it that obvious? I started working out with a trainer and I'm feeling the aftermath," I chuckled.

"Well, good for you and keep it up."

"Thanks"

I continued on to my office. My assistant was trying to hype me up and I appreciated it. Miguel just laughed. Megan and Tim didn't even notice my discomfort. They were in their own worlds. I received several calls from the Millionaire wife who was backstabbed by her sister, adding to their demands. The list was never ending. Don't get me wrong — what the man did was wrong but if she gets her way, he will only have pennies. The worst part would be the custody battle with their twins. After work I headed to the gym. I saw Kyle as I'm heading to change.

"Hey Kelly, ready for another workout?"

"I'm still trying to recover from the first one."

Kyle laughed.

"See you in the minute."

As we began the workout, Kyle asked me some questions.

"So, are you from around here?"

"No, I'm from Chicago."

"Nice, I never been but I hear it's beautiful, except for the violence."

I rolled my eyes.

"What major city doesn't have violence? The media only focuses specific areas."

"OK, OK, now just use that energy for a couple more sets." I gave him dirty look and then laughed. He had set me up.

"You wrong for that and where are you from?"

"I'm from here. I love my hometown".

"So do I and I'm missing some **Harold's Chicken** right now."

"Hometown food are the best places," he said and I agreed.

"You know what I do for a living so, what do you do? he asked.

"I'm an attorney."

"OK, making a note to be careful around you."

I shook my head and we laughed.

After our session finished, Kyle suggested I try a hydromassage to help with the soreness. I listened and it was worth it. I went on my way and headed home after.

The rest of the week involved the divorce case, listening to Miguel trying to analyze me and talk about himself. I don't know why he was trying to figure me out. There was one conversation we had after court when he asked why I had chosen this city and law firm.

"I choose this for my own personal reasons. Why are you so nosey?" I chuckled. "For someone who's all about *me, me, me* you find time to analyze me. Go stare in the mirror." The crazy thing about all of this was that the more he dug the more I got used to it. I even found it funny when I didn't answer. In this case, I just wasn't in the mood.

"It's fun seeing your reaction," Miguel said.

I rolled my eyes.

"OK, now it's my turn to ask the questions. But wait — that's what you wanted all along. Ha! I figured you out."

"Hmmm, but is it the reason?"

"Nope, you will not make me doubt myself. I see you."

"But do you really?"

"OK, I'm done." I walked off.

"Until next time, Kelly."

CHAPTER 5

A few weeks later

Working the case was tiresome but not as tiresome as working out in the gym. I had been sticking to it and was proud of myself. I lost a few pounds. I never understood how men could drop the weight so easily while the fat stuck to women like a clingy ex. It is not fair. Anyway, I went to the gym after work every day. I had gotten used to being around Kyle. He was really good at his job. Also, I couldn't help but stare at him since he was so attractive. I know a lot of women flirted with him. I see them eyeing him while he was training me. They looked at him like they would take all his clothes off and do him right there. He and I talked about things here and there, and we got along. He must have had a girlfriend, or he just played.

One day, as I was leaving the gym and heading to my car, a man tried to talk to me. He looked creepy. He had a smirk on his face along with dark eyes showing scheming intention, while his posture was trying to display approachable. His eyes were giving him away.

"Hey, can I get your number?"

"No, thank you," I said, and kept walking.

"Come on, do you got a man or sumthin? I can be a friend."

"I'm good."

As I walked away the guy grabbed my arm and said,

"If you don't want to give me some willingly, I will take it."

"Let me go!" Panic took me over. This man was strong. I took my gym bag from my other arm and swung it at him. He knocked it away and then grabbed me around my arms and body. I could feel his nasty breath on my neck. I was trying to kick him in balls but I couldn't reach. All of sudden, I heard footsteps and the sound of another man's voice.

"You better let her go!"

I recognized the voice.

"Kyle!"

The next thing I knew, I was released and fell to the ground. I got up and saw Kyle punching the guy and the guy hitting the ground. Kyle continued to punch him. It was like he was consumed with beating the guy to a pulp. The guy was yelling and bleeding more and more. I knew I had to say something otherwise Kyle was not going to stop. I didn't want him to get arrested for my sake.

"Kyle! Stop! Please!" Kyle stopped, looked at my concerned face, got up and came to me.

"I'm sorry," he said. "I... I couldn't stop. I was not going to let that dude hurt you or anyone else."

"I understand. We better call the cops even though I don't want to."

I called the cops. They took our statements and arrested the bloody guy after he got treated. The cops knew him as he was a repeated offender. After they left, Kyle asked me if he needed to follow me in his car to make sure I got home safe. I told him yes as I was still shaken. He followed me home. When we reached my complex, I got out of my car and went up to his vehicle and said,

"Thank you so much. I don't know what would have happened. I mean I do but..."

"It's OK, you are welcome. But we got to stop running into each other in situations like this," he laughed.

"I know!" I laughed. "This is not normal for me."

"Are you sure?" he asked with a knowing smile.

"Yes! The only other creepy encounter I had was a guy looking at me while playing with himself on the redline train back at home." Kyle shook his head in disgust. At that moment Rick James and Teena Marie song *Fire and Desire* started playing on the radio.

"I love that song"

"Well, how about you hop in. I will park and listen to it before you go."

"OK." At this point I knew Kyle and he had saved me twice. I couldn't help but trust him. I got in and he started singing Rick James's part.

"OK, I see you with your vocals," I said.

Kyle laughed. *Damn, his smile is sexy.* Teena Marie part came on and I couldn't resist singing. He just looked at me and nodded. Then we got to the part where they sing together we did exactly that. I even hit the high note.

"Your vocals are on another level," Kyle remarked.

"I actually love to sing," I said, trying to hide my smile, "but I get too nervous to sing in front of people, so only a few have actually heard me."

"Well, I'm glad I got to hear it."

"I guess I should head to my place. Thanks again, I will never forget this". I leaned in and gave him a hug and he gave one back.

"I'm just glad you are OK". I gave him a kiss on the cheek and as I leaned out, he looked into my eyes, leaned in and kissed me. I was in shock yet I couldn't help but kiss him back. We ended up making out. Kyle kissed my neck. I was getting so turned on I wasn't thinking straight and told him to come up with me to my apartment. He said he shouldn't but we didn't stop kissing. I told him again and said, "Don't you want to make sure I get in my apartment ok?"

I got out. He looked at me for a minute and then got out. He followed me and I opened my door. I hugged him and kissed him again. We kissed some more and step inside. I dropped everything and he picked me up with such ease. *Damn, he is strong.* He carried me to my couch and lay me down. He kissed my neck and the center of my chest and I got wetter and wetter. He pulled off my leggings and underwear, and stared into my eyes as he went down between my thighs. Then he kissed my pussy. I let out a moan. He opened up my pussy lips a little bit and licked me. I couldn't help but arch up. He moved his tongue up and down. Then he moved it in a circular motion on my clit. I was no longer thinking of anything. It felt so good. I grabbed his head and arched myself more as I got closer. He stopped for a split second and said, "Fuck, you taste good." He blew briefly on my pussy and I moaned louder. He continued to eat me out, sending me over the edge, and I came a lot. I let out a yell and was shaking. He wiped his mouth and my breathing became steadier. He got up. I was waiting for him to drop his pants but he didn't. He says, "I'd better go." I was confused. I was waiting for the dick. "Did I do something? Is there something wrong with me?"

"No, you didn't do anything beautiful. Actually, would you be willing to go on a date with me?" I was dumbfounded but found the word to say yes. He smiled and said, "How about this Sunday, since you know I work on Saturdays?"

"Sure," I replied, still in a confused state. After that, Kyle left. I was ready to have sex with him right then and there and he didn't even try. This was weird. I wasn't normally that willing. Except I do remember a time I was really close to giving it up on the first date...

* * *

Ammon

I met Ammon after giving Shawn his last chance, when I was 28 and was working at my last law firm. He was half Egyptian and half Italian, with a very sexy accent. We talked and, crazy as it sounds, we clicked instantly. We were talking about everything. The first time we went out we went to this bar and I can't even tell you how long we were there just chatting. Listening to Ammon talk and seeing how sexy he was and I mean SEXY! Light brown skin with jet black neatly combed hair. He had a very sexy smile. He was tall and very well put together. I could not believe I was out with him. I noticed how some women were looking at him. One was even trying to flirt like I was not there but he did not acknowledge her. As the night went on, we moved closer and closer together. Leaning in some more, Ammon asked, "Can I kiss you?" I immediately said, "Yes." When he kissed me, I never felt such an instant connection. We spent a few minutes simply kissing. After we stopped, he wore a big grin and so did I. I was blushing too.

When we finally left the bar, it was icy outside and he was holding my hand. I almost slipped on some ice but he sensed it and grabbed me tight close to him while continuing to walk. On the way to dropping me off home, Ammon never let go of my hand. At each stoplight, he leaned in and kissed me, with a grin that never left his face. When we got to my apartment, we made out in his car. It was intense and got so wet. I'd never thought about giving it up on the first night but I was very tempted. He was holding me close as he kissed me on my neck. In between breaths he had I both said, "We should stop before we go too far". Then we'd go back to kissing. We did stop eventually because he said, "If you don't leave now I'm going to want us to go all the way." I got out and really realized how wet I was. My body was ready for him.

We went out a few more times. We would end up making out and had very close moments of almost having sex no matter where we were. One time, I was with him at his workplace and he had to stay late. He asked me to come by. I got cute for him and went. We ended up making out in his office and I was straddling him on the couch. He was kissing me on my lips, then moved down to my neck and then to my chest. Getting just as wet on our first date. I felt his dick and DAMN it was not small at all. I wanted it. Neither one us had a condom so we stopped. Ammon told me he was glad we stopped because if we kept going he would not have cared about a condom and would want us to go all way. He travelled a lot between Chicago and Atlanta for work. One day when we were together, he revealed something that brought an end to things. He was married. Because he was not from the US, he had married someone to stay in the country. It was an agreement but then his wife fell in love with him. He said he couldn't get out of it until after a certain time period, but she did not want to end the marriage.

We stopped seeing each other because it was hurting Ammon and me since we couldn't take things further. I remember the last day because I knew it was the end. We met up and talked and as he walked me to my car, he kissed my cheek and forehead and said goodbye. My eyes started to water as I got into my car. Ammon closed my door and walked away. I looked up and saw him put his hands on his head and looked up at the sky and then down and heard him let out a big sigh. He paused for a second and then kept walking. I drove off. He did say one thing before leaving: once he was out of that marriage – and if he knew where to find me – he would come to me and make me his woman if I was available. I had moved on since then and never heard from him again.

6

CHAPTER 6

* * *

Friday came and Rochelle, in her usual fashion, asked me what my plans were for the weekend.

"I will be hanging out with the girls on Saturday, and on Sunday I have a date."

"OK Gurl! Tell me about him."

I laughed.

"Well, he is actually my trainer."

"What! How did it happen?"

I told the whole story minus what happened in my apartment. We were not that close. She was in shock and was happy for me. While we were finishing the conversation, I heard Miguel say from the door, "Wow, don't you know how to attract them." He had been listening in. I rolled my eyes.

"Wow, why are you eavesdropping on conversations?" I said.

"Maybe you shouldn't be so loud."

"Ummm, she wasn't even loud Miguel, so try again", Rochelle said.

"Ok, I was about to come in to ask a question when I heard and I did not want to interrupt."

"Uh-huh, you wanted to be nosey as usual. But the question is why?"

"Naw, not at all," said Miguel. Rochelle looked at him and shook her head as she went out.

"What do you want, Miguel?"

"Just want to ask a few questions about the demand."

"Ok, let's focus on that".

Saturday came and I met Lena and Angela at the Mall. I told them everything and they wanted to shop with me for my date on Sunday. Lena and Angela did some shopping too as they had dates in the evening. We went to a couple of places but nothing stuck. It is hard shopping as a plus-size woman. We ended up at Torrid. I did find a Coral dress that looked good on my skin tone. It was fitted, of course, and off the shoulders. I got some Spanx too and found some sandal heels. We went and got manicures and pedicures and then went out to eat.

"I cannot wait to hear about your dates", I said.

"We can't wait either," said Lena.

"Yep, and don't leave anything out. That includes you too, Lena". We all laughed.

Lena was going out with a doctor and Angela was going out with a marketing executive. We went our separate ways after eating. I went home and did my hair since natural hair takes a while to arrange. I called my mom and checked on her. My mom had me in her early forties, so she is older, but my older siblings were nearby if she needed anything. I also chatted with my bestie, Ariel.

Sunday was here when I got up and looked at myself in the mirror. Everything seemed wrong with me. I wondered how Kyle could even want me when he had plenty of options from the lounge to the gym. Then I realized I needed to hype myself up. I decided to play music and put on Lizzo. She was all about confidence, especially for plus-size women. I put that on loud blast. I gave myself some facial treatments and rested. I got dressed later, finished my hair and makeup. I was ready and nervous. Not long after, I heard a knock. My heart jumped. I don't know why I was so nervous. I have been on plenty of dates. I opened the door and there was Kyle looking good. His dress shirt was slightly open and he wore his normal sexy smile. I smiled and said, "Hey."

"Damn, you look sexy."

I smiled. "Thanks, so do you." I grabbed my purse and we left. I asked where we were going but he would not tell me. We listened to some 90s R&B – my favorite decade for music.

Kyle pulled up to a restaurant and stopped at the valet. He climbed out and opened my door, helping me out and holding my hand. We walked in and the place looked beautiful. It had dim lights and looked like an intimate setting. Kyle let them know he had a reservation and they directed us to the table. He pulled out my seat and I thanked him. He was being a complete gentleman. I was still having flashbacks from the other night, and needed to remind myself where I was. We talked about our childhoods. I told Kyle about my very religious family and upbringing. He told me about his family. He is the eldest of four siblings. Which explains why he was always helping people. We were having a great conversation. Dinner was great and after dinner we went walked around the AT&T Discovery District. He took my hands a couple of times and it felt nice. I finally asked the question that had been on my mind.

"Why did you leave so suddenly the other night?"

"What you mean?"

"Umm, well I thought we were going to have sex but you just left."

Kyle grinned.

"I left because if I did stay any longer, I would have ended up having sex with you and I respect you. I didn't want to give the impression that I just wanted sex from you. That's why I asked you out afterward."

"Oh, I don't know what to say. But thanks for viewing me more than just someone to have sex with."

"I know you not the type to just sleep around."

"How do you know that? I mean, you're right, but how?"

"I just do." Kyle stopped and put his arms around my waist, pulling me closer to him. He kissed me gently. I put my hands on his arms and start kissing him back. We kissed for a minute and smiled at each other.

"Just know I did want to be inside you."

I blushed and grew bold.

"I wanted you inside me too".

He regarded me with a surprised look. Like he just realized there might be another side to me.

"OK, I see you."

I laughed.

We continued to walk a little bit before heading home.

When we reached my apartment Kyle walked me to my door. He asked for another date. Of course, I said yes. I asked if he wanted to come in.

"No not yet," he said. I was kind of sad about that response. He kissed me with more passion this time.

"Good night beautiful," he said. "I will see you tomorrow at the gym."

"Good night, Kyle."

I went in and called all my girls, both here and in Chicago, and told them about my date. So far, Kyle had everyone's approval. I went to bed and could not stop thinking about him. I ended up doing some self-love that night, thinking about all things I wanted him to do to me.

The next day came and I never been excited to go to the gym but first I had to get through work. Of course, as soon as I got in my office Rochelle came and asked about the date. She closed the door this time and I told her. Kyle also got her approval. I went to meetings the majority of the day. Later, Miguel found himself in my office.

"Yes Miguel, how can I help you?"

"Nothing just curious as to how your date went."

"Why do you even care?"

"I don't. I'm just curious."

"What does that mean?"

"Nothing but what I said. So, tell me."

"It was great and we are going on a second date. That is all I'm saying. We are not close like that."

"Come on, after all the time we are spending on this case?"

"That does not mean anything. Why don't you concentrate on your dating life if you have one." I knew damn well he definitely had one.

"Wow, I have plenty of women come up to me, and that hurts me a little that we are not friends", he said in a sarcastic tone, putting his hands against his heart. I rolled my eyes.

"Just don't scare him off, OK?" Miguel walked out of my office.

Ugh, why does he constantly have to bother me? What have I ever done to him?

I headed to the gym after work. As I walked in, I did not see Kyle. I went to the locker room and changed. After I came out, I still did not see him. I asked at the desk. They let me know that he was not in today and they had a substitute trainer. Some chick named Torri. She was nice, don't get me wrong, but I wanted Kyle. After I left, I texted him to see if hewas OK. I got no response. My overthinking was kicking into overdrive. *Is he ghosting me? Did something happen to him?* I dismissed the thoughts and left it alone. I would just wait to hear from him.

Thursday came and I had not received any response. On my way to the gym, I wondered if I would be getting a substitute trainer again. I parked my car and as I was walking, I saw that his vehicle wasn't there. I ended up getting Torri again. I really hoped Kyle was ok.

The weekend came and still no word. I decided to text him one more time:

Hey Kyle, I was just messaging you just to make sure you are OK. You do not have to respond if you don't want to but I'm here if you need me.

I already had it in mind that I might not hear from him. I did take into consideration that he was not at work either. I had no plans that weekend and realized I was missing something in my life. Something that I always wanted. So I looked up the local dog shelters and the dogs that were available for adoption. I saw this little puppy that I just automatically loved, and set an appointment. I went Sunday and ended up adopting a Spanador. He was the cutest thing. I went a little crazy with the spending at PetSmart, but it was worth it. I even signed up for dog training classes. I brought my little baby home and got him to settle in as much as I could. I set up his kettle, and his toys and water were ready. I fell in love. This was just what I needed.

On Monday I took my puppy, who was officially named Brownie, to the Doggy Day Care in Petsmart. I went to work and showed off photos of my baby. Rochelle wanted me to bring him. Even Miguel had to admit Brownie was adorable. It kept my mind off Kyle. After the deposition, Miguel was up to his usual antics.

"Why did you get a dog?"

"Ummm, why not?"

"You needed a companion?"

I rolled my eyes as usual.

"Do you even know how to be a companion to even recognize companionship?"

"Of course, I do. I just met a new girl and we're going on a date tonight."

"I bet there are only first dates since I'm sure they realized how self-absorbed you are. After the dates they're never to be heard from again."

"You got jokes, huh?"

"Naw, just truths." This time he walked out. We always go back and forth. What kind of disturbed me is that he kind of reminded me of one of my FWB (friends with benefits). Me and that guy would always go back and forth.

7

CHAPTER 7

* * *

ALEX

Alex was my second FWB (Friends with Benefits). It started after a relationship. Slightly older than my previous guys, he was Afro-centric and a big fan of Malcolm X. We talked on an intellectual level but were always debating each other. Again, I was at a point of not wanting a relationship. We had fun debating but also it was exhausting. He was really cute and tall and light-skinned. We had our hook-ups. We would talk (or should I say debate?) and then say, "fuck it" and hook up. I didn't develop any deep feelings for him but I started noticing that when we talked, he would wrap his arms around me to hold me. He became gentler and cared more about what was going on with me. I knew if we were to ever go down that road it would not work, based on our personalities. Alex did not like white people even though he was mixed, and I was the one telling not to act like that because then he would be just as bad as someone who hates black people. After a while, I met someone and wanted to see where it would go. So, I stopped the arrangement with Alex. I told him to his face and he got mad at me. I asked why — this was just an arrangement. He said he wanted to see where things could go between us. I didn't know what to say. He said he liked me and wanted things to flow and see if we could be a couple. I told him we couldn't. We did not talk for a long time after that.

* * *

I went to the gym, wondering the same questions. *Will he be there? Is he ok? Will it be awkward?* I walked in and I started scanning and did not see him. I went and got changed. I walked out and there he was. He looked at me and smiled. I walked to up him.

"Hey, Kelly. How are you?"

"I'm ok," I replied. "How about you? You have been M.I.A."

"I know. Long story but it does not mean I forgot about you."

"Well, you never texted back, so I just left it alone."

"I know and I'm sorry about that. Let me make it up to you. Let me take you out tomorrow."

"I can't I just got a puppy and I signed up for dog training class. It is tomorrow."

"OK, that's cool. Maybe I will get to meet the puppy soon?"

"Yeah, maybe." We worked out. It was kind of awkward. Kyle

was less social. I did not know what to make of it. When we finished, he walked me to my car. He still did not mention why he was gone but I also did not want to force him. I know what that feels like.

"OK, since I can't take you out tomorrow, how about this Saturday? I'm off."

"Sure, that can work."

"Cool. Again, I'm sorry I did not reply to your text. One day I will tell you why. I just something I had to take care of."

"OK, you don't have to tell me. It's your business."

"I know but if I want to continue this between us, I know I will have to open." Now I really wondered what happened.

"Now, before I let you go, I got to give you one thing." He took me in his arms and kissed me for a minute before letting me go.

"Goodnight beautiful."

I went home. Kyle texted and asked if I made it home after picking up Brownie. I debated about replying since he did not let me know he was OK. I replied because I had a feeling if I didn't he would show up to make sure.

After work the next day, I got Brownie and took him to his first class. I was excited. A few others were already there. There was this guy who I could not help but notice when he came in with his dog. This guy had muscles and a nice beard and nice hair. He looked South Asian. I realized quickly I wasn't the only woman who noticed. All the women's eyes zoned in on him. The trainer came and introduced himself and the class started. I was concentrating on my pup but could not help a glance here and there at the guy. I heard his name was Zain. Of course, his name matched his looks. He saw me looking a couple of times because we made eye contact, and he smiled and I saw his dimples. I looked away immediately. After class ended, I saw how the other women were trying to get his attention. I was not going to make myself look crazy, so I went home. I would see him again on Friday at the next class. I noticed he had a little mystery to him and a few tattoos. A part of me was intrigued and a part of me could tell he was a smooth type. It reminded me of one of my previous relationships.

8

CHAPTER 8

***

Edward

After Shawn, I was still working in the college store while in school. I would travel the CTA train downtown every day. One day Edward came into my world. I just got on the train to head downtown and sat down on the seat getting ready to put my headphones on. A guy turned around with a deep voice and said, "Hey, how are you doing?"

I replied, "I'm fine".

He said, "I would like to get to know you if you don't mind. By the way, my name is Edward".

I looked at him with that smile and knew he was a bad boy just by looking at him. Yet I still said yes as I was young and my confidence was just barely building. I gave him my number and did not write it down. He memorized it.

We started dating after a month or so and, honey, did he bring the drama. While dating I happened to meet Keisha one day who came around to his family's house. She looked at Edward with his arms around me and started cursing at him and me, asking how he could be with me, as if she were the girlfriend. I looked at him like... explain. He said she was just this girl who was obsessed with him. My dumb self believed him. He would write me poetry and make songs for me. I would get random collect calls from jail every once in a while, for being in there for this and that, but he always seemed to get out. Eventually I woke up and realized he was cheating when Keisha kept coming around. I felt used and broke up with him. Later, I heard that Keisha got pregnant by him.

* * *

Thursday came and I went to the gym. Kyle was there and more sociable. I told him about the doggy class minus Zain. I showed him pics of Brownie. He mentioned he used to have a pit bull terrier when he was young. I could see the pain in his eyes as he talked about his dog. I wanted to give him a hug but this was his job and I was a client. Things were getting back to normal but not all the way there yet.

The next day came and I decided to get a little cuter. I took a change of clothes for the dog training class. Comfortable but fitting. I applied a little bit more makeup. Rochelle asked me what was up but I said nothing – I just felt like doing something different. Miguel didn't say too much today, which was weird. I was getting used to our back and forth. I walked past his office and saw him working.

"Wow, you actually know how to work," I laughed.

"Haha! Did you need anything, Kelly?"

"Someone's grumpy today. The date didn't go well?"

"It did go well, and we're even going on a second date."

"Congrats. This is what you call growth."

"OK, Kelly."

"What no smart comments? Are you OK?"

"No, not this time, and yeah I'm good."

I did not know how to handle this side of Miguel.

"Oh, OK, well I won't bother you anymore."

I walked out and attended the dog training class after work. Everyone from the last session was there, and then came in Zain, looking just as good as before but with a fitted t-shirt and sweatpants. I could not help but look at the pants to see if I saw an imprint. Of course, while I tried to look discretely the other women were making it very obvious. I noticed they were showing more than they were in the first class. I wore slightly more fitted clothes but I did not show my assets as if I were in a club. I wore my leggings with a long fitted v-neck top that went just past my butt. I was not going to be desperate. Just like the class before I took a peek every once in a while, and again Zain would catch me once in a while too. He would flash that smile and I would look away and try to hide my smile. I hoped he would not see. One of the moments happened and as I looked away, I noticed one of the women stared at me in disgust. I rolled my eyes and let it go.

After class, as I was heading out I felt someone walking up next to me. I realized a dog on a leash had come up and was getting close to my puppy, like they wanted to play. My eyes grew wide for a second and my heart started pounding as I knew whose dog that was. I turned my head to the left and there was Zain now next to me. He smiled and said,

"Hi, you have a cute dog. My dog seems to want to be friends with yours."

"Yeah, it seems that way. Your dog is adorable."

"Thanks. My name is Zain, by the way." His deep voice was getting to me.

"My name is Kelly. Nice to meet you." We were outside at this point. I was heading to my car.

Zain followed.

"Hey, do you ever go to the dog park not too far from here?"

"No, I haven't. I'm new around here so I'm still learning about all the places."

"Well, since our dogs are getting along, how about we do a play date for them?"

I laughed.

"I'm pretty sure there are others who are wanting the invitation." I tilted my head in the direction of the group of women looking at our interaction. I saw the anger in their eyes. Zain laughed.

"Yeah, but I'm not interested. And also my dog picked your dog."

"Uh-huh, ummm I'm free on Sunday."

"Sunday it is."

We exchanged numbers. He wished me goodnight and to staysafe. I got Brownie into the car and drove off. My mind was going into overdrive as usual. *Is this a date? Or is this just strictly a playdate for our dogs?* Obviously, I would not have that answer right now. My mind flashed back to the women who were looking at me hatefully. It reminded me of my first FWB.

9

CHAPTER 9

***

William

After getting out of a relationship with Shawn (the first time we broke up) I did not want to date for a while. Facebook was becoming really popular at this time, when it was just for college students. I was on it and started a group. One person at my university joined and began messaging me. His name was William and he was FINE! I looked at his friends list and saw he was friends with one of the girls in my class who had the same major as me. We knew each other. I asked William how he knew Tina.

"Oh, that is my cousin," he had said. In my mind, I was like, yeah right. In class the next day, Tina came up to me and said,

"My cousin William asked about you." I was in shock. I mentioned how we were in a group together on Facebook. She said he was majoring in culinary arts and that's why I never saw him. I messaged William about him asking about me. After some back and forth he decided we should meet.

We met on campus. As I saw him walking up, I quickly realized he was better looking in person. He had a dark caramel tone and was very tall with a smooth vibe. We talked and got along really well. We started to hang out more and I noticed something. As we would walk around campus together, other girls would look at me with disgust. Like what was he doing around someone like me (I wondered the same thing myself). Clearly, other girls wanted him. Just when I thought he couldn't get more attractive, he showed up on campus one day in his Air Force uniform, walked up to me and gave me a hug like normal. I smelled his cologne... lust was starting to build inside me for him. The girls really hated me that day.

One day we were hanging out in one of the common areas. At this point we were friends. William was talking about his back and neck hurting, so I offered to massage his neck and shoulders. He accepted. I was massaging his neck when he blurted out, "You might not want to touch there, that is my spot." That threw me off guard for a moment, but I brushed it off. I continued to massage and touched the spot again, then he said, "touch it one more time and we going to end up fucking." I laughed it off again not taking it seriously. I touch it again and he got right up and said, "Let's go."

I laughed but then I saw his face.... he was serious. "You are kidding right?"

"No." He took me in his arms and kissed me. I got so turned on. I did not know what was happening or how it was happening. We got on an elevator and he took me in his arms and started kissing with more passion. We somehow found an empty classroom and we made out. He was touching me all over and I could feel his big dick through his pants. He pulled my shirt up and pushed aside on side of my bra, exposing one of my breasts. He started licking and sucking on my nipple. I couldn't help letting out a moan. He was grabbing my butt and pushing me more into him. I do not know how but we realized we did not have protection so we stopped ourselves. Afterwards we talked and realized this was officially beyond friendship. I did not want a relationship due to my previous experiences, and neither did William. So, we agreed to be FWB (friends with benefits).

I will say William was the one who opened up my sexual side. He had me doing things I never did before. His was the first dick I sucked, and I even tried anal (keyword.... tried). It was not for me. We had fun. Our arrangement eventually ended when he wanted to give his ex another chance. I understood and we remained friends. Little did he know I started to like him more but I did not tell him then. I felt he might have not noticed. It did not come out until later while we were talking about something on the phone. I had said, "I can't believe I really liked you" and I chuckled. There was silence on William's end and then he said, "Why didn't you tell me?" I said we had an agreement and I did not want to make things weird. He asked again and then said, "I liked you too." I was dumbfounded. We didn't talk about it again as he was not available. We eventually stopped talking and he married his ex. One day, a couple of years down the line, William called me out the blue and mentioned how he and his wife were separated and that he wanted to be with me. I told him no because he was still married and I did not want to be in the middle of it. After that, I never spoke to him again. He sent a text one day, saying, "Hey, how are you? I was just thinking about you." I knew not to reply, so I blocked him.

* * *

Later on that night I got a text from Kyle. He was advising me to dress comfortably as we would be outside and walking a lot. Also, he told me to be ready by 9 am. I wondered where we were going. I prepared for the next day. Angela wanted to spend time with Brownie anyway, so I arranged for him to stay with her. I got up early the next day to get cute for this date. I twisted the front part of my hair and let the natural be free. I wore torn Bermuda shorts, a blue tank top, sunglasses and a small over-the-body purse. I dropped off Brownie and went back home. Kyle showed up not too long after. He came to my door like before, wearing shorts and a tank top.

"Hey beautiful, you ready?"

"Yep, just let me grab my purse."

"Where is your puppy?"

"He is with my friend. She wanted to spend the day with him."

"Oh, I was hoping to meet him."

"Well, he is my child and you don't get to meet him that fast." We both laughed.

We got in Kyle's car, but again he refused to tell me where we were going. We ended up on the expressway and talked about each other jobs. Of course, his job got drama from the lounge side. We were in the car for a while and he let me know we were almost there. I looked around. From the expressway I noticed roller coasters, and the upcoming exit said Six Flags. I asked if that was it and he confirmed it. I was excited.

When we got there, he opened my door and I gave him a hug. He kissed me. I told him I had not been to Six Flags amusement park for years. I went to one outside of Chicago. I used to go every year with my family, and even went with my friends sometimes. We went on every ride and he even won me a stuffed animal. I almost got sick on one ride and held me just to make sure I was OK. I did find that sweet. We spent the whole day there. He was constantly putting his arms around me when we were waiting in line. A kiss here and there. People would have thought we were boyfriend and girlfriend and not on a second date. After we left, we went out to dinner. We were laughing and talking about the day. When he dropped me off at home, he walked me to my door, as usual, and kissed me while holding me tight.

"I had fun today," I told him.

"I'm glad you did, and so did I."

"Did you want to come in?"

Kyle chuckled.

"Not tonight but you will know when I will be."

"OK, OK, well goodnight, Kyle."

"Goodnight, beautiful."

Again, Kyle made me do some self-love that night. Ugh, why does he got me waiting? Usually, it is the other way around. The next day came and I got a morning text from Kyle and Zain.

Kyle:

Morning Beautiful. I had fun yesterday and want to plan another date soon. I will call you later.

Zain:

Morning. Are we still on for the playdate today?

I replied to Kyle first:

I had fun too and yeah, give me a call later.

Then I responded to Zain:

Yeah, I'm still down for that just let me know where and what time.

I sat on my bed and realized that I was attracted to two guys at the same time. I knew where Kyle stood, but didn't know what Zain was thinking. When I went to pick up Brownie, Angela pretty much told me she can take him if I ever did not want him. I laughed but told her nope, Brownie is my baby. I went home, and by the time I got back I received a reply from Zain letting me know the place and time in the early afternoon. I got myself ready and did the wash n' go hairstyle with big hoops earrings. I noticed my body was toning up a little bit so I decided to wear a wrap crop top and high-waisted jeans. I got a text closer to the time from Zain saying he was heading there. I grabbed Brownie's items and leash. He got real excited, and I could not help being nervous and excited myself.

We reached the park and got Brownie out. I texted Zain, letting him know we were here. He called me right after.

"Hello?" As I started to look around.

"Hey Kelly, where are you right now?"

"I'm in the parking lot, heading to the entrance. Where are you?"

"I'm near the entrance. I'll come towards you."

"OK." As I said that I spotted him and – oh my god – he was too fine! He had on a fitted tank top that showed off his muscles. He had on shorts, sunglasses, a fresh, lined haircut and a stubble beard.

"I see you," Zain said. I hung up and he gave me a hug. Damn, his cologne smelled so good!

"How are you?" I asked.

"I'm good. Glad you could make it. Dakshi was excited."

"So was Brownie."

"We reached the area where the dogs could run off the leash. We let them go and they both sprinted off. We were watching them play when Zain turned to me and said,

"You look pretty today". I was not ready for that.

"Thanks, and what? I was ugly the other times in class?" We chuckled.

"Of course not. You looked sexy then too."

I froze for a second trying to process what he just said. I just ended up blushing and said, "Thanks and you're not too bad yourself."

"Thanks."

"Just don't let it go to your head," I laughed.

"Naw, I'm not like that. I wasn't even like this when I was younger."

"What do you mean?" As I tilted my head in confusion.

"I used to be ugly and bullied, even." I was shocked that came out of his mouth. Looking at him, I would have thought he always been attractive.

"I don't believe you."

"It's true. I was made fun of for my acne and weight."

"Oh wow, I'm sorry you went through that. It's never a good feeling. I know where you are coming from.... Sort of.

"OK, my turn. What do you mean?"

I smiled.

"I can't say I was bullied but I was invisible to the other kids and boys never really said anything to me except when they wanted my help to talk to my friend."

"You sexy though. Boys are stupid."

I smiled again and looked away. We talked about where we were from. His family was from Pakistan. He was an entrepreneur. He owned a couple of restaurants. We both came from religious backgrounds but both of us are spiritual.

"What made you ask me to this playdate?"

"It was an excuse to ask you out but since you brought that up maybe I can take you on a real date, if you let me."

Internally I screamed as this beautiful man asked me out. "Sure, we can go out."

"Great! How about we go to the dinner and a movie tomorrow?"

"Tomorrow would not work as I go to the gym." The thought of Kyle came to mind. *Should I go on this date when things are going well between me and Kyle? We are not in a relationship though. We'd just been on two dates. I'm still single so I can go on other dates.*

"OK, how about Tuesday evening?"

"Yeah, Tuesday would be great."

We played with our dogs for a while. When it was time to go, we got our dogs and walked to the parking lot together. I felt a connection to him like he understood my struggles growing up. He was a gentleman, and conversation flowed. We said goodbye and hugged again. He told me to let him know when I made it home. Which I made sure to.

Later in the evening, I received a call from Kyle.

"Hey, Kyle."

"Hey, beautiful. Are you free to talk?"

"Yeah, I'm free. I was just preparing for tomorrow."

"OK, cool. I wanted to invite you to my place Tuesday, and I will cook dinner for you." Immediately Zain came to mind.

"Ummm, Tuesday would not work but I'm free Friday evening."

"OK, that would work for me too."

"What will you be making?"

He laughed.

"You'll have to wait and see."

"I guess," I laughed.

"How was your day, beautiful?"

"It was good. I took Brownie to the dog park on a playdate."

"Brownie already has a friend?"

"Yeah, from the dog training class."

"Oh nice! We should go together one day."

Immediately in my mind I was like NO.

"Sure, what did you do?"

"I didn't do anything important. Just did some cleaning and laundry. Also, did some errands."

"So, basically adulting."

He laughed.

"Yeah, adulting..... I really like you, Kelly," he said out of nowhere. "I just want you to know that."

"Aww, I like you too, Kyle. You have been there for me twice already and we enjoy each other's company."

"Exactly. What are you doing this second?"

"Nothing. Just lying down. I will go to sleep soon. What are you doing?"

"I'm also in bed, thinking about you and wishing I could give you some right now."

"You had opportunities before."

"I know... I just wanted to do things right by you. But it does not change the fact that every time I'm at your door a part of me wants to take you inside and undress and give you some head and dick. Just make you cum multiple times."

I was getting turned on.

"Why are you telling me this now?" I felt myself getting restless and thinking about him.

"I can't hold back anymore. I want to feel you. I don't think I'll be able to hold back on the next date. I also get to see you tomorrow. I got to fight the urge to take you in my arms and kiss you and feel on you. Damn baby, I want you". His breathing was changing. Like he was stroking his dick.

"Kyle... are you touching yourself?"

"Yeah, baby. I can't help it. Thinking about you is not help-ing."

It was turning me on more. I pulled my pajama pants down and then my underwear. I started to feel on my nipples, thinking about Kyle touching them. I was starting to feel myself. My breathing was changing.

"Baby, are you touching yourself?"

"Yes, look at what you are making me do."

"Mmmm, finger your pussy, baby." I rubbed my pussy slowly and found my clit. I started flicking it. "Mmmmm it feels so good Kyle. I want your dick."

"Take this dick, baby. Imagine me putting it in slowly and taking it all in."

I opened my drawer next to the bed and took out my dildo.

"Mmmm, it feels so good. Fuck me please."

"I'm fucking you baby." I rubbed my pussy then put my dildo inside me. Going in and out. We were both making noises and I felt it building. "I'm getting close."

"So am I baby. Fuck! I'm about to cum, baby. FUCK!"

"Ahhhh, I'm cumming." I starting shaking and felt myself cum. At the same time, I heard him cum.

"Mmmm, baby. I can't wait to give it to you in person. I'll let you get some sleep; it's late."

"OK, goodnight, Kyle, and thanks — I needed that."

"I needed that too, baby. Night." I cleaned up and went to sleep.

10

CHAPTER 10

The next day at the office, it was business as usual, except Miguel was still acting a little different.

"What is wrong with you?" I asked him while we were going over some things.

"What do you mean?"

"You have not been making your usual smart comments. You have been surprisingly reserved."

"I just didn't feel like doing that."

"Umm, OK." I let it go and went on with my day.

Later on, at the gym, Kyle was giving me more "attention". Even when he was helping me do reps he would feel on my legs and I would look at him and smile, and he would bring his head closer like he was going to kiss me but pulled back and continue training. I whispered, "I wouldn't want to get you in trouble."

He chuckled. "Naw, you good. I'm trying to stay professional but it's hard right now." This went on the whole time of subtle touches. When we finished the session, he said, "I'd leave with you but I got another client. Let me at least walk you to your car."

"Ok," I replied.

We walked and when we reach my car and put my gym bag in and closed the back door and all of sudden, I felt Kyle grab my arm and turned me around, and pressed me against the car with his body. I felt his dick pressing against me and it was hard and definitely not small. He looked in my eyes and then leaned in and kissed me softly at first, which then turned to passion. He wrapped his arms around me while he continued. After what seemed like a couple of minutes, he let go and said, "Goodnight beautiful, let me know when you make it in." Then he just walked off and back into the building. I was at a standstill, my lower half wanting attention.

The next day, the workday seemed to go fast. After work, I had to rush home and get ready for my date. I started to feel like I was cheating on Kyle even though we were not boyfriend and girlfriend. I pushed the thought out of my head and got ready. I freshened up my curls and put on my pink mini dress and leather jacket with some wedges. I heard a knock, and as I opened the door Zain was there looking FINE as Hell.

"Wow, you look gorgeous, Kelly."

"Thanks, and you look very handsome."

"I'm alright." That just got him more points — I do like a man who doesn't know how fine he is.

"I'm ready". As we left, he opened the car door for me and got in. We drove to the movies. While there we listened to some old hip hop and even some pop music. We were dancing all the way there. We got to the movie theatre and he bought the tickets. We talked a little bit before the movie started. We talked about our childhoods more. The struggle of being the invisible ones. We seemed to understand each other. He mentioned how he got bullied daily at school and he eventually got fed up and started training and fought back. I told him about the time in 7th grade a boy asked me to be his girlfriend as a joke. The movie started. Not too long after he pulled the usual move of putting his arms around me. I could not help but look at him and smile. After the movie, Zain took me to his restaurant for dinner. You could tell the restaurant was high class. We talked and laughed. We compared the war stories of our dogs. We even had a couple of discussions about our exes but it was brief. I was liking him. At one point he put his hand on my hand and I felt goosebumps all over. We enjoyed dinner, and when he dropped me off he walked me to my door.

"I really enjoyed our date, Kelly. I'd like to take you out again."

"I enjoyed it too and yes we can go on another date."

"Glad to hear it." He moved closer and asked, "Would you mind if I give you a kiss?"

"Ummm, sure." He leaned down (as he was around six feet tall) and kissed me. I felt a warmth come over me. I kissed him back. "I will see you tomorrow at the class."

I don't know how I mustered the word but I said, "OK."

Zain smiled and left. I was now heading toward a state of confusion. As of then I was attracted to two guys at the same time.

The next day when I arrived at work, there were flowers on my desk. They were beautiful, red, pink and purple flowers. I wasn't in my office for two minutes and Rochelle came running.

"Things must be going well with the trainer!"

I smiled as I looked at the card:

Hello Gorgeous,

I hope you enjoy your day.

-Zain

The shock must have been written all over my face because Rochelle came over and looked at the card.

"Soooo, who is Zain?"

"Welllll, it's a guy who I went on a date with yesterday."

"Where did you meet this guy? And what happened to Kyle? And what does he look like?"

I laughed.

"I met him at the dog training class. I'm still going on dates with Kyle. He is around six feet. He has muscles and jet-black hair. He has a sexy smile with dimples."

"What nationality is he?" I was trying to not make that a factor.

"He's Pakistani."

"WHAT?! OK gurl, I see you tasting different flavors."

"I'm open to all races and nationalities and ethnic groups. If there is a connection, why would I judge them on that?"

"Nothing wrong with that all! I'm happy for you. You having your fun."

"I'm single. No one claimed anyone."

We talked about the date and went on throughout the day. Miguel still was not back to his normal self. He was in my office discussing work, and he just kept looking at my flowers like it was bothering him.

"Why are you looking at the flowers like that?" I asked.

"Like what?"

"Like they did something to you."

"You got jokes."

"What is going on with you? You have been acting different. I know we go back and forth but I'm not mean. Is everything ok?"

"Yeah, nothing is wrong. It was just my way of welcoming you."

"Ummm... OK."

After work I went to the dog training class. As I arrived the vibe was slightly different. The other women who were trying to get Zain's attention were staring really hard at me. Some with disgust on their faces. The other women looked at me as if they weren't sure whether they should talk to me. I ignored them. Then Zain came in. I knew this was going to be interesting. Brownie immediately got happy and wanted to run to Zain's dog. Zain came up and said, "Hey gorgeous, how was work?" He gave me a hug.

"It was good. I had a surprise when I walked into my office. Thank you."

"You're welcome, and I'm glad I could help." I gave him another hug and he kissed me on my cheek. I peeked to my right and saw the women's mouths drop in disbelief. I just smiled. The trainer started the class after that. Afterward, Zain and I walked out together.

"So, when are you free next? asked Zain.

"Let me think. I will be free Sunday."

"OK, why don't we make a day of it? The dog park for our dogs and then in the evening just us."

"OK, I like that."

Zain gave me a hug and kissed me on my cheek, then a peck on the lips before telling me goodnight. Right before I got in the car, I noticed the women looked shook. I went home and slept well that night.

Friday came, and after work I went home to get ready for my date with Kyle. I wore a simple flowing dress as I was just going to his place. He wanted to make dinner for me and have a movie night. When I reached his place, he had to guide me where to park. He helped me out of my car and immediately took me in his arms and kissed me. It felt good. When I reached his apartment. It had a modern look. I loved the exposed brick look.

"You have a nice place."

"Thanks! Well, you can either hang out on the couch or at the table in the kitchen."

"I will hang out in the kitchen."

"Cool."

We talked for a bit while he cooked. I tried to help but he would not let me. I will say he looked like he knew what he was doing. He looked good doing it too. When finished he got some wine out and we had dinner. Music was playing in the background and our legs were rubbing up against each other. After dinner, we went on the couch and put on a movieclassic, and of my favorites, *Coming to America* with Eddie Murphy. I could recite it, line by line.

We both loved it and were laughing. I felt him getting closer and then he turned my head toward him and he leaned in and kissed me lightly. Then came another kiss and another. He put his hand to my face and caressed me. He then started kissing my neck. I was getting turned on. Then he moved his hand down to my chest and was lightly rubbing my nipple through my dress and bra and turning me on even more. He got up and I saw his bulge through his pants. I was getting wet. He took my hand and pulled me up. He continued to hold my hand as he directed me to his bedroom.

Kyle took me in his arms and started kissing me again. He was holding me close as possible to him as he went back to kissing my neck and licked it. I let out a soft moan. He unzipped my dress and let it drop, and at that moment I was just in my bra and underwear. He took off his shirt and let his pants drop. He just had boxers on. I could not help but look at him all over and he was sculpted to perfection. He looked at me and said, "I want you, Kelly". He kissed me with so much passion I did not know what came over me. I put my arms around his shoulders and my hands on the back of his head and kissed him back. I was pressing my body on his. His kisses accelerated from my mouth to my neck, then to my chest. He pulled down the left side of my bra, exposing my left breast, and he took my nipple in his mouth. I felt his tongue flicking it. As he was doing that, he unhooked my bra took it off. He switched to my right nipple and did the same thing. My breathing grew ragged. He then picked me up and laid me down on the bed. He took off his boxers and there it was: long, upright and ready. I wanted it bad. I looked up into his eyes and saw lust. He climbed onto the bed and started kissing me all over my body. He pinched my nipples lightly and sucked on them. Then he gently rubbed my pussy through my underwear while keeping my nipple in his mouth. I moaned more and got even wetter.

Kyle pulled off my underwear and then leaned over and grabbed a condom from his drawer. He put it on and moved on top of me. I felt his tip at the entrance of my pussy. I spread my legs further apart for easier access. He entered and felt his thick dick driving slowly into me. I felt this tingling feeling all over and said, "Give it me, Kyle. I want all of it." I heard him grunt and he went in further. I gasped. He started stroking me slowly. I held on to him, digging my nails into his back as he was going in and out. "Fuck baby! You feel so good," Kyle said. He increased speed a little bit. He had me moaning louder and louder. I arched myself as he put his hand on my breast and licked my nipple. He got faster and harder, and at one point I was about to scream in pleasure. I yelled, "Don't stop Kyle! Fuck, don't stop!

He kept going and I heard him grunting more. "Shit baby, I'm about to cum". I said, "I'm... about... to..." and I let out a yell and he did a final thrust and held it there and yelled, "Shit!" We were both breathing hard. "Damn baby, you felt so good." He held me for a little bit and eventually we fell asleep.

The next morning, I woke up and he was not in bed. I relived last night in my mind and I could not do anything but smile. I sat up and smelled food. *Wow, he is cooking breakfast too.* I saw a hoodie and put it on. I'm glad I'm only 5'4" so it was long enough to go past my butt. I went into the bathroom and looked at my-self. My hair was all over the place. I tried to freshen myself as much as I could since I did not want him to see me looking crazy. He gave it to me good last night. It had me thinking twice about giving Zain a chance. I walked out and into the living room and at that moment my heart started beating fast.

11

CHAPTER 11

I was not ready. I could not believe what I was seeing. I saw Kyle and a girl I recognized from the gym. She was one of the employees. They did not see me as they were sitting on the couch and it was facing away from me. Also, despite having some weight on me I'm light on my feet. I backed up a little and just listened.

"Look Kyle, I know we had a lot of issues but I want to give us another chance. I miss you and you were going to be my husband."

My heart dropped.

"Nicky, you messed that up, not me."

"We can work on it. Just give us another chance. I know you still love me. Also, if I didn't have the miscarriage, we would have had a child". Then she leaned over and kissed him. He did not push her away.

I knew at that moment I needed to leave. I went back into the room and put my clothes on. I was glad I left my purse near the door. I quietly left the bedroom and reached the entrance. As I picked up my purse my keys fell. I picked them up and looked up. Kyle and Nicky looked at me. Kyle had the look of shame and I was horrified. I just opened the door and left. I heard Kyle call my name but I just ran. I took the stairs and heard him again but I did not turn around. Thank god for the remote start because I could not face him right now. I turned on my car and got in. I pulled out just in time as he was about to reach me. I drove off and saw him through the rear-view mirror, standing there. Tears were coming down as I replayed what was said. They were engaged and they see each other every day. And he hadn't pushed her away when she kissed him while I was just in the other room naked. I had to let him go.

When I reached home, Brownie met me at the door. I dropped everything and held and petted him. Kyle left several missed calls. I lost count of how many times he tried. I saw texts popping up but could not look at them. I was happy that my girls were coming over later on to hang out and drink. I needed that. I got myself together and took Brownie for a long walk. I was listening to some music and got the place together. When Lena and Angela came, they saw something was wrong. I got our wine and waited for the food we ordered. I told them everything. They comforted me and reminded me that even though things are not working with Kyle, Zain was in the picture too. I was feeling tipsy when we heard a knock on the door. Food had arrived. Angela went to the door and opened it. Then I heard his voice and sobered up... a little.

"Please let me talk to her."

"Naw," Angela replied, "she doesn't need this right now."

"Please, I just want to explain."

Angela looked at me and I shook my head.

"Sorry, not tonight." She closed the door.

Lena turned to me: "I'm sorry gurly, he should not have shown up."

"Ugh, ok I need to get drunk. Wait — I can't get that drunk 'cause I'm supposed to go out with Zain tomorrow."

"Well, focus on that and not Kyle," said Lena.

"You right," I said. "I just was really liking him and after last night, it did not help."

"Of course, he gave you some, and it sounds like he took care of you," said Angela.

"Yeah...ok, fuck it, let's get the focus off me and drink." We finally got our order and laughed and talked. We even played some games and talked about random things. I needed this. They crashed at my place and I made breakfast in the morning before they left. Then I got ready for Zain.

When I met up with him I kind of still had a headache from drinking. He was waiting for me and gave me a hug and kiss on the cheek. We let our dogs loose.

"Nice sunglasses," Zain said.

"Thanks, it's very sunny and I might have overdone it a little last night when I was hanging with my girls." We both laughed.

"At least you had fun and with good people."

"Yep, that is true."

"How was your evening?"

"It was good, spent time with some friends and relaxed."

"Nice!" I took off my sunglass and let my eyes adjust.

"You are really attractive, you know that?" said Zain.

"Me? I'm alright."

"You are more than alright." I smiled and blushed, but internally I had mixed feelings as Kyle popped into my head. We went and played like before with the dogs, and after we dropped them off at home Zain let me know we would go to dinner and then to a botanical garden. I got cuter and he picked me up for the evening. On our way to the restaurant, he took my hand and held it. He was making me feel special but in the back of my mind I wondered, *why me*? He could literally have any woman he wanted.

We arrived at an Italian restaurant. Zain was a gentleman throughout. We talked about almost anything and everything. After dinner we walked around the gardens and, as I expected, they were beautiful. He held my hand as we walked. We even took selfies, and he would wrap his arm around my waist to pull me close to him. Again, his cologne smelled so good. We continued to walk for a little bit and then he stopped me. He put his arms around me and kissed me with passion. His tongue find mine. We ended up making out for a couple of minutes and it felt so good.

"I've been wanting to do that all evening," he said.

"Well, I'm glad you did," I replied.

Zain smiled and caressed my face. "It's getting late, let's head back to the car."

We walked back and he took me home. At my place he parked and we ended up making out again for a little bit before he walked me to the door. "Have a good night Gorgeous." Not too long after getting home, he sent me a text message:

I just want to say I enjoyed our date and I enjoy spending time with you. I just want to know if you wanted to have another date?

I texted back:

I would like another date. How about this time, I will cook a meal for you? At my place?

I wanted this to be different. He responded quickly:

Zain : Yeah, I would like that. When are you free next? I already decided I was not going to the gym tomorrow or maybe this week.

Me: I'm free tomorrow or Thursday.

Zain: Tomorrow works for me

Me: Ok, tomorrow it is. I better get to bed. I got court in the morning.

Zain: Ok, Night Gorgeous

The next day I got flowers again. Actually I got *two* sets of flowers: one from Zain and one from Kyle.

The note from Kyle said:

I'm sorry, please give me a chance to explain.

The note from Zain said:

Can't wait to see you tonight

Rochelle came in and said her two cents. The one response that had me looking confused was from Miguel. He came in and said, "These guys can't send anything different or send it to your place?"

"Why do you care, Miguel?"

"I don't."

"Well, then don't act like."

He just walked out.

Rochelle came in and closed the door, then walked over to my desk and whispered, "You know Miguel is into you?"

I laughed and shook my head.

"No, he isn't. He's into himself."

"Gurl, with the guys you are pulling, you don't know when someone is indirectly interested in you." I did not want to believe her.

"Stop playing Rochelle. He is not into me."

"OK, don't believe me."

Nope, Miguel was not into me. Also, that wouldn't be allowed. What is crazy though, is that I do remember there being a guy in college whom I was blind to.

* * *

The one I will never know

It was while I was working in the college store. I interacted with a lot of other students. I was moving my way up in a management role. So, I would handle certain things. I became really close friends with one of my co-workers and we understood each other. She understood my insecurities even though she was pretty and skinny. We are still close to this day.

She started to tell me about this white guy that would come into the store and wait to make sure he got me when I was helping at the registers. She told me how he would have a big grin on his face. Later she would tell me how she tried to find excuses for me to come if I wasn't there. I didn't believe her because white guys never took an interest in me. I brushed it off. It was not until further down the line that I started to notice how he would just smile at me. I always ended up helping him since I handled everything for veterans like him.

I started to realize how really attractive he was. I told myself, *No he is not into me.* One day he came to get a textbook, but it was out of stock. I let him know I would order the item. It was slow that day and I was playing '90s R&B at my desk. I apologized and told him I would turn it down. He said I did not have to; he liked the artist. I was surprised that he knew them since they were not one of the popular ones. That made me start to notice he had a little swag. We talked a little. His item arrived and he happened to stop by. His telephone number was listed on the document.

"You could have called me, I would not have mind," he said. I was speechless and just smiled. Later one day, when he was about to graduate, he came in to get his cap and gown. We had a little small talk and flirted a little. That's when I started to realize maybe he was into me. After that, I did not see him for a while.

Then, I got offered a new job at a law firm and it was in my major. I had to take it. I did not get to see him before I left.

Not too long after I left the store, I stopped by to visit. I asked if that guy ever came in. The girl who replaced me said yes, and that he asked for me. She just laughed and told him I didn't work there anymore. Ugh! I felt like that girl was a hater. The thing is, I took a small shot and put my name and number on a small piece of paper in the book I ordered for him but I did not put it in an obvious spot, so I'm pretty sure he did not see it. After what the girl told me, I knew I would never find out if he wanted to take me out.

12

CHAPTER 12

***

After work, I went to the store to get items and picked up Brownie. Back at home I started cooking lasagna. I changed clothes and had just finished getting ready when there was a knock on the door. I opened it. Zain was standing there, holding more flowers and looking good.

"Hey Zain, come on in."

"Thanks, and I know you have flowers at work but I also wanted you to have them at home."

"Aw, thank you." I gave him a hug and a kiss. I put the flowers on my dining table.

"Dinner will be ready soon. Make yourself comfortable."

"Your place looks nice", he said as he sat at the table and played with Brownie.

"Thanks, I'm still putting things together." I laughed.

"You need any help?"

"No, it is actually just about finished." I noticed my phone was ringing. It was Kyle. I'm pretty sure he was calling because I did not come to the gym today. I ignored it. I finished up and we had dinner while talking about our day and having deep discussions about religion and politics. We truly had an understanding.

"This is really good, Kelly."

"Thanks, I appreciate that. I will have to cook some soul food one day... I mean if we are still talking."

"I don't see a reason why we wouldn't be. I'm really into you, Kelly. I'm drawn to you. I know it only our third date but I hope we can eventually be together as boyfriend and girlfriend."

I was in shock and just blushed. Right after I heard a knock.

"I'm not expecting anyone else." I went to the door and opened it. It was Kyle.

"Kyle, what are you doing here?" Kyle stepped into my apartment and said, "Please just let me explain." And at that moment he saw Zain.

"Kyle, I don't want to talk and as you can see, I'm on a date. Please go."

"I'm sorry for barging in. Just please give me a couple of minutes."

"Dude, she said she does not want to talk," Zain said.

Kyle turned to him. "I was not talking to you; I'm talking to her so stay out of this!"

Zain got up and walked towards me and Kyle.

"It's time for you to go."

Kyle got closer to Zain and you could see the anger building in Kyle.

"STOP, just stop! I said, as I tried to separate them. I felt a panic attack coming on. My heart started racing and I stumbled back. Kyle and Zain caught me. Zain then picked me up and took me to my couch.

"Are you OK, Kelly?" Zain asked.

"I will be," I said breathlessly. "I think I just had a panic attack."

"Let me get you some water". There was a scared look on Kyle's face that I have never seen before. He said, "I'll leave. I don't want anything to happen to you. I'm sorry."

After that, he left.

"Who was that guy, if you don't mind me asking?"

"It was someone who I was talking to but not anymore."

"He fucked up?"

"Yes, he did."

Zain brought the water and I started drinking it.

"Well, his loss for messing things up with a beautiful woman." I smiled.

"I'm sorry the date got messed up."

"Don't be, baby. The date isn't over, plus there will be others."

"You're right." We relaxed on the couch and even made out for a little bit. Zain was feeling my thighs as we were kissing and even grabbed my ass. It was getting hot but after all that happened we both knew we weren't going to have sex that night. Despite the earlier drama the date ended well.

As Zain was leaving, he paused for a second and looked at me.

Caressing my face he said, if that guy ever bothers you again, let me know." He took me in his arms and gave me a passionate kiss. "Goodnight, gorgeous."

After he left, I planned for the week ahead. I had to decide if I would change gyms or stay but change trainers. After thinking, and having a few more sips of wine, I decided to stay at the gym but without a trainer because, after going for a while, I can keep it going on my own and could even convince my friends to come with me. The gym was too convenient for me to change. I sent text messages to both Lena and Angela, asking if they would join me at the gym.

The next morning. I got a few text messages. Angela and Lena were on board for the gym. I got a good morning text from Zain. Also, a text message from Kyle. Kyle's message said:

I wanted to say I'm sorry for everything. I know you don't want to talk to me right now but I just want you to know you impacted way more than you know. I can guess I won't see you at the gym or don't want me as your trainer anymore. Just let me know. Hopefully, one day we can talk.

I responded:
You are right I do not want to talk right now. I do not want you to be my trainer anymore.

I proceeded to get ready for work. By now I knew what to expect. Flowers from Zain were on my desk, which always put a smile on my face. The day went by fast. I was dreading the gym but here I was, waiting outside for my friends. I looked inside and saw Kyle. I was just hoping he would not see me. I waited a few minutes and looked back in and....Oh no, he just saw me! *NO NO NO!* It looked like he was about to come towards me but then my friends finally showed up. I looked back and he had turned around again.

"Hey! Sorry we're late. Traffic was horrible," said Lena.

"It's OK. You guys just made it on time. He saw me but then he saw you guys."

"Glad we made it then," Angela smiled.

We went in and got changed. Honestly, working out with my friends was great. We were laughing and talking about everything. It helped me not think about Kyle. Even though I saw him a few times and he had this pleading expression on his face, I just turned away. The workout was a success and now that I was with my friends, I felt I could come here on a regular basis.

After work the next day, I saw Zain at the dog class. This time, he came up and kissed me on my lips. I felt the laser beam of eyes on me from the women across the room.

"Hey gorgeous, how was work?"

"Too long. How about you?"

"The same but at least the day can end well." I blushed and he smiled.

The class went quickly and the trainer let us know that we only had a few weeks left for class and graduation.

"Aww, no more classes together," I moaned.

"It's OK, I get to take you out more."

"I like that." I then leaned against him, pulled his head towards mine and kissed him. Out of the corner of my eye I saw one of the women's mouths drop open before she walked away.

We went to the car where I got a hug and a more passionate kiss. We planned to go out Friday. Zain said his usual goodbye, making sure I let him know I made it home. He went to his car. I had barely sat in my seat when a few of the women came over to me.

"How did you do it?" asked woman number 1.

"Do what? I said."

Number two rolled her eyes.

"How did you get that guy?"

"I did not do anything. He came up to me."

"No. You had to give him something or do something for him to be interested in you."

Even though I knew the answer I asked the next question anyway.

"Why would I need to do anything?"

"Because... you know...you are...."

"What? Overweight? Well, that's what you get. You assumed you knew what he likes. I'm not going to waste my time with this." I got back into my car, closed the door and drove off.

When I got home, I messaged Zain, letting him know I made it home. He called after I sent the message.

"Hey gorgeous, ummm I saw how the women came up to you and I saw the anger in your face. Is everything ok?"

"Yes, I'm ok. They just pissed me off."

"What happened?"

"I don't want to bother you with it."

"You're not, babe. What happened?"

"Well... they came up to me and asked how I got you. Like they could not believe you are with a woman like me."

He chuckled.

"Wow, they are sad. It is none of their business. They are not you."

"Why *did* you choose me? They were definitely trying to get your attention."

"I wasn't drawn to them. Also, I could tell they did not have any real substance. With you I didn't just see an attractive woman. I could see you were more than that. I had to get to know you. I'm glad I met you."

I was silent for a second.

"Thank you, I don't know what to say."

He laughed.

"You don't have to anything."

We talked a little more and then I knew I'd better get to sleep. Zain was proving to be a great guy. But I was still nervous about our growth.

The rest of the week was a blur and then came Friday. I brought my change of clothes with me to work as Zain was coming to get me from work. Rochelle insisted on hanging out after hours to get a glimpse of Zain. We were going to the movies in the park. I missed those. I use to do that back home. Zain was bringing the food, and I brought the hidden alcohol. After I got changed, I talked with Rochelle for a little bit. The receptionist called to tell me Zain had arrived, so Rochelle and I walked to the front and there he was, in his t-shirt and jeans.

"Hey gorgeous". He came over and kissed me. I turned to look at Rochelle. She had the biggest smile on her face and gave a nod of approval.

"I'm sorry," I told Zain, "this is my assistant, Rochelle. Rochelle this is Zain, my date."

"Nice to meet you, Zain. Now I know who been sending flowers."

He laughed.

"Yeah, well she is worth it."

"Uh, yeah she is. And remember that."

"I will." As the two of them were talking, I saw someone off to the side. It was Miguel. Once he realized I was looking, he left. I just blew it off and went back to Zain and Rochelle.

"Well, you two have fun. I need to hurry up before my man gets mad. I know he been waiting."

"Alright, Rochelle. See you Monday," I said.

"OK, and nice meeting you, Zain."

"You too."

Zain and I went on our way. We found a good spot and observed the crowd growing around us. We would be watching, the classic, *The Breakfast Club*. We had a great time reciting the lines with the crowd in various scenes. Zain was holding me most of the time, and it felt great. After the movie, we hung around to let the crowd die dissipate. We talked and kissed a lot. We eventually left and arrived my apartment. He took me in my arms and kissed me deeply with his hand caressing my face. He then wished me goodnight and left.

13

CHAPTER 13

A few weeks later...

The case was wrapping up and things were moving along. Kyle had left me alone and I had been going on quite a few dates with Zain. After one particular date, we came back to my apartment. I put my bag down and asked if he wanted anything to drink. He declined, then came up and grabbed me, taking me in his arms. He started kissing me intensely. He scooped me up and put me on the kitchen counter but never took his lips off mine. His tongue found mine. Standing between my legs, he pressed his body against mine. His kisses left my lips to my neck. He kissed and licked softly. I grabbed his hair and moved my head for easier access. I felt his hands rub my back then caress my thighs. He removed my top and kissed me again. He unhooked my bra and took it off and tossed it somewhere. He fondled my right breast and moved his thumb lightly in a circular motion on my nipple and grabbed my other breast and did the same thing at the same time. Then he left my lips again and took my right nipple in his mouth and was sucking and licking my nipple. I moaned. He switched breast and put his thumb back on my right breast and sucked on my left. I was getting so turned on. I took his shirt off and felt his chest. I kissed it. He picked me up and carried me to the bedroom.

He put me on the bed. I watched him unbuckle his belt and take off his pants. He had on boxer briefs, but seeing his imprint got me wetter. He pulled off my jeans and then my underwear. He kissed my left inner thigh and then my right inner thigh. He went to my pussy lips and gave it one long lick that sent me over the edge.

"Mmmm, you like that babe?" he purred.

"Yesss."

He licked it again and opened my pussy lips and licked some more, and when he got to my clit he licked even more. He sucked on it too. I could not help but grab his head and put my thighs around his head while begging him not to stop. "Don't stop Zain, please don't". He kept going and I felt myself getting close. I was pushing his head. I think I was suffocating him but I would not be able to tell. "Mmmm,I'm about to cum." I arched up and released. He was taking all my juices. He got up from in between my thighs and I saw his dick was hard and ready. "I want your dick now, Zain." He gave a sexy grin.

"I want to give you this dick."

"Give it to me now. I want to feel it inside me."

I leaned over and pulled out a condom. He put it on. He climbed on top of me and slipped his tip in and moaned instantly. With each stroke, he was putting his dick in more and more. I felt his cock all the way and I started to meet his slow thrust.

"Fuck babe, your pussy feels good." Zain was going in and out, and I felt every inch. He was feeling too good and I wanted to take over. I pushed him back and he looked confused. I winked at him and I pulled him to the side of me and I got up and straddle him. When he figured what I was about to do, a smile spread across his face. I took his dick and put it inside me slowly. He moaned. I started going up and down slowly. He put his hand on my hips and then started feeling on my thighs and back to my waist. I started to ride more and moved my hips in a circular motion. We both moaned. Feeling his thick dick inside felt so good. I started to increase speed. He sat up a little bit and started sucking and feeling my nipples again.

"I'm getting close, Zain."

"So am I babe. Damn, Kelly."

I smiled. He was meeting each thrust and it sent us into overdrive. I screamed while he grunted and we came together. He held me so tight and I felt his dick throbbing as he came. He caressed my face and looked into my eyes as our breathing became normal again. He put his hand around my neck and kissed me. He lay me down and I put my head on his chest. He held me. We fell asleep.

I woke up before he did and slowly got out of bed. I freshened up in the bathroom and put on my silk robe. I checked messages while deciding what to make for breakfast. I chose turkey sausage and French toast. While I was cooking, Zain emerged in his boxer briefs only, and said, "Good Morning."

"Morning. I hope I didn't wake you."

"No, you didn't. Mmmm, what are you making?"

I told him and asked if he wanted eggs too. He did, and as I cooked he came up from behind, wrapped his arms around me, kissed my neck and gave me a hug.

"Thank you for making breakfast."

"You are welcome. I'm just about done." I asked him to get the plates and set up the table. He did just that. I made the plates and drinks and started to eat.

"This is good babe."

"Thanks!"

"Kelly?" I looked at him and he had a serious look.

"Yes?"

"I wanted to ask if you would like to my girlfriend."

I looked into his eyes. I saw the sincere look and then I knew my response.

"Yes, I'll be your girlfriend." I smiled and so he did he. He got up and kissed me with so much passion.

"I'm glad we are officially together. I don't want anyone else," he said.

"I feel this connection between us that is very strong and I feel safe with you," I replied.

"Good because I feel it too and I want you to feel safe."

We finished eating and cleaned up together. Zain then loosened up my robe and kissed me and put his hand inside my robe and caressed my body, my waist and then my ass. He grabbed my ass and squeezed it. His kiss intensified and I backed up to my couch and he followed. I lay down and he got on top. He lowered his underwear and he entered me and I gasped. He was kissing my neck while going in and out. He looked into my eyes and I kissed his lips and bit his bottom lip. He moaned and sped up his rhythm. I grabbed his shoulders and wrapped my thighs around his waist and grabbed his ass, begging him not to stop. He was going faster and harder.

"Shit, baby, whose pussy is this?"

"This....is.... yours." As I was taking a breath in between. I return the question, "Your dick belongs to who babe?"

"It's yours, baby.... all yours." I gave his neck a lick and he went faster and we knew we were about to come and he did a final thrust and we came. We got up and took a shower together. Afterward, he had to go handle some business, but before going he kissed me and let me know he would call later.

Once I was alone I picked up my phone and rang my childhood bestie to give her an update on what happened. After that, I called Lena and Angela on three-way. I told them what happened and that I'm off the market.

"I'm so happy for you!" gasped Lena.

"I second that!" We have to all go out with our men," said Angela.

"Yeah, I agree. We've got to plan it. OK girls, we got to figure out when everybody is free," said Lena.

"Yeah, I'm down for that," I said.

"I'm down too." We talked a little bit more and we would follow up with each other.

I did some cleaning and took Brownie for a walk, then ran some errands. While out I got a text from Zain.

Hey babe, I just wanted to say I'm glad you became my woman. Last night and this morning were just wow. I'm missing your body right now. Also, get used to me spoiling you. I know you are independent and I love that about you but I also love to give things. I hope you are having a good day and will call later on in the evening.

I couldn't help but smile and I could not get rid of it. I knew I had to reply back.

Awww I'm glad you are my man and last night was great and you know how to reach me. You want to spoil me? That's sweet and look forward to knowing exactly what you mean by that. Hope you also have a good day babe.

I got ready for the work week and watched a show on Netflix. I did some online shopping too. As I was getting ready for bed, Zain called and we talked about each other's day.

"Hey, would you want to go on a group date with my friends and their men?"

"I don't mind babe. As long as I'm with you, I'm good."

"Cool, which day? Friday or Saturday?"

"Saturday would be better. I got a couple of private parties I got to check in at both restaurants on Friday. After I do that I was hoping I could spend time with you?"

"Oh. What do you have in mind?"

"Well, I want to cook you an authentic Pakistani dinner and for dessert... you already know."

I smiled.

"I love that. I guess I better bring some things, and if Saturday is a go for our group date I might as well stay over for the weekend. If you don't mind."

"Of course, babe. I'll make room for you in my closet."

"I will do the same for you."

"Glad to hear it. Side note — what did you mean by 'spoiling' me?"

He laughed.

"You'll see babe. Just be patient."

"Fine." I chuckled. We talked for a little bit more and said goodnight.

The next day I got my flowers as usual. Rochelle did not take long to talk about Zain.

"You know what I'm here to talk about...what's his name again?"

I laughed.

"Zain."

"Right! So, how are things going between you two?"

"It has been really good. In fact, we just became a couple. So you'll probably see more of him."

"For real? Yasss gurl and congrats! He is FINE AS HELL!"

"Thanks, Rochelle. And yes, he is." We laughed and went back to work.

Later on, Miguel came into my office to finish up things for one of the cases.

"So, how are things with your men?"

"I see the old Miguel is out and I don't have men. I have a man."

"So, you've chosen?"

"If you asking if I'm in a relationship now then yes, I'm. But something tells me you knew that."

"That is a big assumption."

"Uh huh."

"So, who is the victim?"

I rolled my eyes.

"Why do you care? Also, what was that about a few weeks ago?"

"What do you mean a few weeks ago?"

"You were hiding around the corner while I was I with Rochelle and my then date." I smirked, thinking about Zain.

"Well, I was not hiding. I was doing something."

"Really? Cause I saw you looking and then you left."

"I was about to leave and I saw you guys. I wanted to know if that was a potential client you were trying to get behind my back."

I shook my head.

"I know you're lying because I'm pretty sure you saw him kiss me, and I was in regular clothes. What's going on Miguel?"

He scrunched his face up and got up and walked towards the door but then turned. He looked at me and said, "Dammit Kelly, I know Rochelle noticed because she been teasing me but you can't see?"

"See what?"

Then I remember what Rochelle said about Miguel. *No No No. Please no. This can't happen. He is my colleague and I have a man. I don't even like him like that. He is too conceited for me.*

"Nothing, Kelly". Miguel had a frustrated look on his face and walked out. A part of me was curious but a part did not want to know.

14

❧

CHAPTER 14

I met up with my girls after work at the gym. While we were working out, I saw Kyle walk past. We made eye contact. When he turned towards me I turned my head away. I looked at my friends and they saw too. I knew what they were asking without saying it. Did I want to dip? I shook my head because I can't let him chase me out. I looked back and Kyle was getting closer. All of a sudden, the girl named Nicky came up and jumped playfully on Kyle and kissed him.

"Ummm, was it her who was at his apartment?" asked Lena.

I looked at Lena and Angela and nodded.

"Aww, hell naw!" Angela groaned.

"We're done anyway. Let's go," said Lena.

We got our stuff and went to the locker room. As we walked away, I could feel Kyle's eyes on me. We talked about the group

94

date. Everyone was available for Saturday and wanted to go to a lounge. A great excuse to get sexy and great music. What came next, I was not prepared for. The girls wanted to go to the same lounge we went to the first time we went out.

"Wow, you guys would do that to me knowing Kyle works there?"

"The only reason we want to go is that it's reggae night. Also, you will be there with Zain. Show Kyle what he lost," Angela said. I shook my head but she wasn't wrong. And I did love reggae. I agreed. I knew I had to look good that night.

The next day was the graduation for the dogs. When I got there, I was in the classroom waiting and seeing the women looking at me with their usual angry faces. Zain came in.

"Hey babe, I missed you." He kissed me and squeezed my ass. We smiled at one another.

"I missed you too."

The trainer started the final class. The graduation ceremony was cute; the dogs got their little diplomas. Afterwards, Zain held my hand as we walked out.

"Hey babe, so they have decided we're going to the lounge so we can go dancing. It's reggae night. I love reggae!"

He laughed.

"I'm fine with that. I can't wait to see you dance. The way you were moving your hips the other night shows you know how to wine."

I give him a wink.

"You'll find out when we are there and maybe after." Then I

put my arms around him and he did the same, and we kissed passionately. I felt his tongue dancing with mine.

"Damn babe," Zain said, "you better go otherwise neither one of us is going home anytime soon."

I laughed.

"OK, babe. I'll let you know when I get home."

"Please do, babe."

I got in and was driving towards the exit and I saw the group of women from the class looking one last time. All I did was laugh.

The next day I did some shopping after work, and got a manicure and pedicure. It was a self-care evening. The rest of the week was so-so, then I packed on Thursday for the weekend as I would be staying over at Zain's. I was bringing Brownie too.

After work, I picked up Brownie and drove to Zain's place. When I arrived, he grabbed me as soon as I got out of the car, and lifted me up while giving me a kiss. I loved the fact that he could pick me up. We entered his condo. He took my stuff to the bedroom and I let Brownie play with Dakshi. Something from the kitchen smelled really good. Zain said he was making chicken tikka and chana chaat. It looked really good. He poured me some wine while he cooked and talked. Once dinner was ready, we fed our fur babies and ate ourselves. After, he got up and left for a second and came back with a smile. He looked like he was up to something.

"What is going on? You look like you are up to something."

He laughed, moved his seat closer to me and handed me a

box. It was a jewelry box. I opened it and saw a beautiful bracelet inside. I was in shock and looked back and forth between him and the bracelet.

"Well? Do you like it?" He asked.

I snapped out of it.

"Yes, of course. It's beautiful. You didn't have to get me this."

"I know I didn't have to, but I wanted to. I said since we are together, I will spoil you."

"Thank you, babe." I leaned over and kissed him. He kissed me back. He caressed my face and started kissing with more eagerness. I was kissed from lips to cheek to my neck; he then licked and sucked lightly on my neck. I squirmed in my seat, feeling turned on. He stood up while still sucking on my neck. He pulled me up and went back to my lips while holding me close to his body. He was rubbing my back down to my ass. He stopped and took me to the bedroom and closed the door so we could be alone.

He sat at the end of the bed, and I sat on his lap, facing him. We kissed some more, then he went back to my neck and then to my chest. He pulled off my shirt and then I took off his top. I put my arms around his neck. He was holding me, my legs around his waist. He got up and was about to lay me down on the bed, but I wanted to do something. So I released my legs and stood up. He looked at me and then I pushed him down on the bed. I climbed up and kissed him on his lips before lightly biting and sucking on his bottom lip.

Then I caressed his chest and kissed the center of it. I move down to his left nipple and sucked it, then switched to his right and bit it slightly, looking at him as I did it. I could tell he was getting more turned on. I smiled as I moved off the bed, unbuckled his pants, pulled down his zipper and removed his pants. I tossed them aside. Then I took off his boxers. His dick was already hard and ready. I took it in my hand and licked his tip. He moaned. I licked it again and before taking the tip in my mouth and licking and sucking his head while massaging his balls. I took more of his dick in my mouth and sucked on it more, licking it all over. Then I took more. And more. I started moving my head up and down and I looked at him. He was leaning his head back and making eye contact with me. I did not stop looking at him for a minute. He was moving around.

"SHIT, babe. That feels good." I found a sensitive spot. I licked it and he jerked. "FUCK". Zain grabbed my head as he moved his hips. I went back to licking that spot and he lost it. He grunted, "Fuck babe I'm about cum." I did not stop. He held my head there and came into my mouth. He was jerking. I took his dick out of my mouth and swallowed his cum. He looked at me, then lifted me up and kissed me.

Zain took me down on the rug and pulled my leggings and underwear off. He spread my legs and apart and licked my pussy. I moaned. He came up and kissed me while rubbing my clit. He then took one of my breasts in his mouth and licked and sucked and switched to the other breast while rubbing my pussy. I felt myself getting soaked. He then went down and licked and sucked on my clit. I was grabbing his head and then I felt myself getting close but then he stopped. He smiled at me. He stayed on his knees and pulled me by my legs closer to him, and he entered me. He started out slow. I was in heaven. He stroked me slowly so I felt every bit of him. While stroking me, he kissed me and sucked on my neck. I was holding on to him. Begging him not to stop. "Right there, babe. Mmmm." He started to go faster but then pulled out and turned me around so he had me on my knees, and he put it back in from behind. Doing me doggy style. I felt him going faster and harder. We were both moaning. His hands were on my waist and our hips were moving together, meeting each other's thrust. The sound of our skin slapping together was making us go faster. I yelled out. We knew we were about to cum and we both yelled when we came. Zain held me while pushing his waist against me as far as he could. I felt him throbbing. He held me like this for a second before letting go. He then got me up and put me in bed. He climbed in and we just stroked each other's body and kissed and fell asleep.

15

CHAPTER 15

This time I woke up alone in bed. I got up and put on my robe. I checked myself and went out of the bedroom. I found Zain in the kitchen feeding the dogs.

"Morning babe," I said.

"Morning gorgeous. Did you sleep well?"

"Yes I did, thanks to you." I smiled in a devilish way.

He came up to me to with a smile and kissed me.

"I'm glad."

"I hope you slept well?"

"Oh yeah, I did. I want to take you out to brunch, babe."

We went to a café and just relaxed. Afterwards, we took the dogs out and just chilled. Later on, I let Zain know I was going to get ready and would be straightening my hair. He told me he had never seen my hair like that. I laughed and let him know that he would see how long my hair actually was, and that it took time. He left me to my own devices while he went to his restaurants to handle some business. I jumped in the shower, straightened my hair and made sure my dress and makeup were set up. When he came back he walked in and paused for a second. He looked shocked I laughed.

"Wait – your hair was at your shoulder and now it's past your chest?"

"Yeah, curls are tight and cause shrinkage. It's black girl magic," I chuckled.

It crossed my mind that Zain might ask me to keep my hair straightened all the time. But then he said,

"It looks beautiful, but so are your curls."

"Awww, thanks, babe." I kissed him.

He jumped in the shower and I got dressed. I put on my gold one-shoulder bodycon dress and put on my makeup. I put on the bracelet and gold dangling earrings. Zain paused again and looked at me up and down and I was doing the same to him. He wore dress pants and a blue button-up shirt with part of his chest showing — basically looking sexy as hell. He came over and kissed me for a long minute.

"Damn babe! You going to end up making me have to fight tonight."

I chuckled and shook my head.

"You funny babe."

"You think it's a joke? I see how some guys look at you when we are out and in that dress? They will try."

I blushed.

"Please, they will be other pretty girls there."

"Well, there will be no one like you." He kissed my forehead. We finished up and left. I called my girls and they were on their way too. This is the first time they would be meeting Zain. I was kind of nervous because Lena and Angela were the "Hot Ones", but I would eventually know if he could be swayed.

We reached the lounge and pulled up to the valet. Zain got out and came for me. He took my hand into his and kissed it. Lena, Angela, and their men were already in the VIP section. As we walked towards them, I looked around to see if Kyle was there but he wasn't. A sigh of relief poured out of me. We entered the booth and. I immediately hugged my girls, all of us complimenting each other. We each introduced our men. Angela and Lena's men looked fine as hell, as expected. Angela's man is Korean and has a slim build but has muscles. Lena's man is Irish and tall who is a gym rat and always where tight clothes. When I introduce Zain, Lena and Angela gave me a look of approval. It's great to communicate without words. We sat down and ordered drinks from a waitress. She was flirting with Zain but he simply gave her his order then asked what I wanted. She finished taking the order and left in a huff.

I was starting to feel the music. Looking at me, Zain wrapped his arms around me and kissed me on my neck. I could not help but smile as I touched his arms. He whispered in my ear, "Damn babe, the way you're moving is making me want to lay you right here." I play-hit and kissed him. We got our drinks and ordered a few more. Zain continued being touchy-feely and I was loving it. He nibbled on my ear and I chuckled, but I sensed that someone was looking at me. I felt a nudge from Lena. I looked up and saw Kyle. He was across the floor, standing just a little above the crowd and looking directly at me. I knew I better maintain my composure. I looked at Lena and she shook her head. Angela picked up the vibe and looked up and saw him too. He kept staring at me and then at Zain. He seemed almost jealous. I turned away and ran my finger down Zain's exposed chest. Zain looked up from my neck. I kissed him and he caressed my face. He whispered, "You better stop before we at it in this lounge." I smiled while I looked into his eyes. My hair fell across my face and he moved it behind my ear and kissed me again.

Angela announced she needed to go to the bathroom, and of course, me and Lena were going too. I looked back and saw the guys talking. As we got close to the entrance of the bathroom, I felt someone take my hand. I turned and saw Kyle. He had a pleading look on his face. "Kelly, come talk to me for a second." I shook my head and took my hand back. Angela and Lena stood between us and we all headed into the bathroom.

"I can't believe he came up and took your hand," Lena said, shaking her head.

"He had the audacity to ask can yaw talk," said Angela. They both shook their heads.

"I should not have come here," both of them said in unison.

"Fuck him," Angela said. "Plus you have Zain and he is FINE! And so is your man, Lena."

"All of our men are sexy," I said.

"Yep, and we know how to attract them," Lena grinned. We

all laughed. We freshened up and went back out. Lena and Angela were my bodyguards from Kyle. I saw him but did not come any further. We returned to our men and got them up and dancing. I had Zain's hand and we headed into the crowd with our friends. A "Gyptian" started playing. I loved that artist. I wined against Zain while facing away from him, and he was loving it. I was moving my hips and leaning against him. He leaned down and grabbed my face and kissed me. I bent over a little and twerked a little bit. Zain was holding on to my waist. I turned my head to look at him and he looked into my eyes and then my ass. He pushed himself against my ass and moved his hips. I knew what would be happening tonight when we got home. I leaned back against him and moved my hand behind his head. He kissed my arm I continued to wine.

My girls were hyping me up as they danced with their men. I was hyping them up too. I looked a little to my right and noticed Kyle staring angrily in my direction, though not *at* me. Then I realized he was looking at Zain. I'm glad Zain was occupied on my hips. I turned around and faced him. I danced with him and we were moving our hips together to Sean Paul's song. He placed his finger under my chin and lifted my face and kissed me with so much passion. He then spoke into my ear: "You are going to make me put you against the wall and fuck you." I smiled and kissed him, then said, "Oh yeah?" He took my bottom lip into his mouth and sucked on it.

We danced for a while and I turned him on more and more. Eventually Zain busted out, telling the group, "It was really nice to meet all of you but we got to go." He looked deep into my eyes and knew what that meant. He wanted me *now*. Angela, Lena, and I looked at each other and we all knew what that meant for us. We laughed. We headed out and at the corner of my eye I saw Kyle looking. The valet brought Zain's car and opened my door. As we drove, Zain started rubbing my thigh and then his hand moved to my pussy and he started rubbing my pussy through my underwear. He looked at the road and then me and went back and forth. He started rubbing more and my breathing grew faster.

"You're so beautiful, Kelly."

I spread my thighs wider and started moaning. I leaned back in the seat. He did not stop and I was moving around, my moaning increased.

"Fuck baby, listening to you just gets me harder." He knew I was getting close and he stopped. I looked at him like what the fuck. He smiled. He said, "That's what you were doing to me in the lounge. I wanted to lift your dress and push your panties to the side and do you right there on the dance floor."

Zain arrived at his place and parked his vehicle. He switched off the engine and moved the seat back. I could not take it anymore. I went to the back seat and pulled him towards me. He did not hesitate and as he got in the back, he grabbed me and I straddled him. We were kissing and he was feeling me all over. I pulled up my dress and pushed aside my underwear while I unzipped his pants and we maneuvered ourselves. I pulled out his dick and I put it inside me and I moved my hips. I said, "This is what you wanted babe, to move my hips on your dick."

"Fuck yes baby," he said. On the side of my dress that did not have a shoulder strap, he pulled out my breast and sucked on it. It made me ride him more, feeling his dick going inside and out; him kissing me all over and holding me tight. "Fuck baby, this pussy is mine. No other man will have this pussy."

I said, "This dick that's in me right now is all mine. No other woman will have this."

"You damn right, baby." I moved faster, going up and down, and we were making a lot of noise and the car was moving. We were both cumming, and he held me so tight and bit my neck a little bit. Good thing I was on birth control because I would have gotten pregnant this weekend. After we got ourselves together, we climbed out of the car. My legs were a little weak. Zain noticed and fetched my flats that I had left in the car. He took my heels off and put on the flats. We looked around and noticed there was a camera high up on the wall. We looked at each other and laughed before entering his condo.

We were greeted by our pups. Zain heated some leftovers and went to bed not long after. When I finally woke up, I felt him lightly caressing my face. He smiled at me and said, "Good morning, beautiful." I greeted him back. We talked about how last night and we stayed in bed for a little while before eventually getting up to make food. We chilled for a little while, walked our dogs, and then I headed home so I could get myself ready for the week.

16

CHAPTER 16

When I got home, Angela, Lena and I did a group call.

"Gurl, I'm tired," Angela said.

"Me too," I agreed.

"Me three," Lena said. We were silent for a second and then we all laughed.

"I guess we all got some," I said.

"Yeah," Angela and Lena said at the same time. We couldn't help laughing.

We talked about our men, and after we got off the call I continued getting myself together. The next day came I got an edible arrangement for Zain. Rochelle, who was too geeked for it, wanted some. Of course, I said yes. The rest of the day was uneventful except for texting and sexting Zain all day. I canceled working out as I still hadn't recovered from the weekend. I went home and ordered food and watched some Netflix. I heard a knock on the door. I was not expecting anyone, but Zain was now my boyfriend and could show up anytime. I opened up the door and was not ready for who I saw.

"What are you doing here?" I said. There he was again in front of me. Kyle had the nerve to show up here. He came right in.

"I had to come to see you, Kelly. I can't get you off my mind and every time I see you. I just want to take you in my arms."

"Well, it does not matter. We're not talking anymore."

"Kelly, please just let me tell you what was going on. Then I will never bother you again."

"Fine. You got two minutes."

"Nicky and I use to date and even got engaged. We got engaged after she got pregnant. I wanted my child to have a family. She had a miscarriage and after that, we had more issues than we had already. She ended up cheating on me and we broke up. She just showed up at my apartment wanting to talk that morning. I did not ask her to come over. I don't want her. I want you." I shook my head.

"Well, one: I was in your bed, and we just had sex the night before, yet you let her in while I was there. How am I supposed to feel about that? That's insulting to me. You couldn't wait until I left to do that? Two: she kissed you and you didn't fight it. She kissed those same lips that had been on me — I who was still in your place. I asked you to leave while I was on a date, yet you could not do the same!"

"Aight, I give you that. I shouldn't have let her in but we were not boyfriend and girlfriend either."

"Of course, we were not. I never said we were. It was about respecting the fact that your date was still there, someone you just had sex with, and that another woman was in the same space. Plus, I saw you guys kiss! If you don't understand that, that is your problem and not mine." Brownie started barking. We both looked at him and then Kyle looked back at me.

"Come on Kelly. You know we're good together. We are better than that dude you brought in the lounge. I wanted to punch him. The way he was all up on you. I wanted to break his arms seeing how you were rubbing your ass on him."

"Look at you! You getting mad at me for being with a guy in your presence, but I'm not supposed to get mad at Nicky being around while I was there. Hypocritical asshole! Remember, you're not my boyfriend but guess what? That guy you saw? He just became my boyfriend, so I'm no longer available." I saw anger fill Kyle. He came towards me, grabbed me and kissed me while holding me tight. I was trying to push him off me and then I slapped him. He backed up.

"Damn, at least I know you the loyal type. But you should have been *my* woman, not his!"

"Get out Kyle! Your time is up."

"I'll leave but if he ever fucks up or hurts you, let me know."

Kyle finally left and I locked the door. I calmed Brownie down and heard another knock. I was about to snap now. As I opened the door I said,

"I told you to leave so get..." I realized then it was not Kyle but Zain. Zain came in and had a very angry look on his face.

"Why was that guy here?"

"He was trying to talk me again."

"How many times has he come here?"

"He hasn't come since the last time you saw him. He was at the lounge and saw us and apparently felt compelled to come here. I made it clear I don't want him and that you are my man."

Zain eased up a little.

"I'm glad you made that clear." He kissed my forehead. "I came to surprise you." He stood there for a second silent and I saw his hand ball up into a fist. "I'm going to find that guy and beat the shit out of him."

"Babe, forget him. I don't want you to go to jail over this. It's not worth it. You have me, babe. Only you." I went up to him and put my hand on his face and made him look into my eyes. He calmed down more and I moved his head so I could kiss him. He put his arms around me and we started kissing. He held me tight and he was kissing me and he took off my shirt and then his. We moved to the bedroom. He tossed me on the bed and he dropped his pants and boxers. He pulled him off my pants and underwear. He got on his knees and he started rubbing my pussy with one hand and pinching my nipple. He was kissing my chest and my stomach. While rubbing my nipple he started to lick my pussy. He took his tongue and moved it up and down and in circles. I was moaning grabbing the sheets. He increased his speed and started sucking and I started jerking and he held my hips and he was eating me out and I came fast and hard. He licked up all my juices.

He stood up and said, "This is my pussy right?" and I said, "Yes, it is babe. All yours." He got on top of me and he entered me and he was doing long strokes. He took my hand into his and he was grabbing the sheets. He was grunting and looking into my eyes. He then sucked on my neck and was licking. He then kissed me deeply. He started to increase speed and pounded harder. "Fuck baby, you are my woman. Fuck!" He started grunting more and going harder, and I was holding on to him and biting his shoulder slightly as I was coming. He thrust hard and deep in me like he was making sure all his cum was in me. He held me there for a moment with his head on my shoulder. "I'm falling in love with you," Zain panted. My eyes got wide and took his face into my hands and looked at him in his eyes to make sure he realized what he had said. He looked at me and kissed me with passion.

"Ummm, babe was that the sex talking or is that how you really feel?" I asked.

He looked at me and caressed my face. "I meant it. You are an incredible woman. I care about you. I only want you. I don't want anyone else. The fact that a guy was trying to take you away from me... I wanted to fight him. I want to protect you and I'm always thinking about you, always wanting to make love to you."

I kissed him. "I'm falling for you too."

We kissed for a while. Zain decided to stay over. He fell asleep. I was thinking about our relationship. I was realizing he was really a good man and I did not want to jeopardize things. It made me think of a previous relationship I had.

* * *

Rueben

This was the guy for who I decided to break my second FWB for. We met at a Starbucks downtown of all places. Rueben was tall, with a football player body, and had dimples. He was in school and studying accounting. We just clicked in a way. He always made sure I was good. He made me feel wanted. Like I was worthy of a relationship. We both had fathers who were in the military, and we were both the youngest in our families. I even got real sexy for him one day and pulled the Beyoncé-type of music video of "Dance for You" vibe. The issue we had was arguing. He had a bad habit of saying whatever came to his mind, and sometimes that harmed our relationship. It reminded me of my father in a way that was not good. The sex was great at first, him being able to lift me up, etc. But then it wasn't. The more we got into it the more I fell out of love with him. I broke it off after three years. He didn't want us to end. He wrote poems for me. One day after we broke up officially, he asked to come to Starbucks where we met. I asked him why but he would not say. I refused and he blurted out saying, "I was going to propose to you." I did not see that coming, especially as we had broken up already. The more I look back at this relationship the more I realized he was a good guy and this was on me.

17

CHAPTER 17

* * *

<u>*A few weeks later.......*</u>

It was the weekend and I spent the majority of the morning walking Brownie and catching up with the people from Chicago I was still in contact with; just trying to get all my errands done before spending the evening with Zain. Not too long after I got home I heard a knock on the door. I looked through the peep-hole and stepped back. I was on my way to a having panic attack. Brownie was barking non-stop, and I backed up until I was able to lean against the wall. *It can't be him. How did he find me? I left him in Chicago. Why is he here?* I heard the knock again. I refused to go to the door. "I know you in there. I saw you come home. Please open. I just want to talk. I'm sorry for everything. Just talk to me. I came all this way," he pleaded. I still didn't move. He knocked again. "Please open the door." All I could do was think back to what drove me to leave Chicago. He was the reason. Jason was the reason.

* * *

JASON

I met Jason through the religion I grew up in. I was 30 and working in one of the top law firms in Chicago. I decided to give it another try my previous relationship. I had been at a get together at one of the church member's home, minding my own business when Jason, who was with a friend of a friend, approached me. He was attractive, and the other women in the organization were fighting for his attention. His caramel complexion was matched with light brown eyes and he had a nice build. Jason attended a different congregation. We talked for a little bit and exchanged numbers. We went our separate ways because people make assumptions if you hang around members of the opposite sex by yourself. Later we texted back and forth. I learned that Jason grew up in the religion too and he left for a little bit and came back. He became really active in the religion. Having been around these people my whole life I knew that even though he was very 'active', he was not truly all in mentally. I was kind of happy about that because some people take it to another level of devotion and become judgmental to the max. Jason was baptized but I still was not. I was happy I was not forced to. My parents allowed me to make a choice, while some people I know were forced into it.

Jason and I talked and, even though we were not supposed to, we went on dates without a chaperone. We were supposed to let the elders know too but then it would be a problem as I was not baptized and we are only supposed to date baptized ones and, along the way, decide if we wanted to get married. Jason understood every struggle with the religion, and I didn't have to explain myself. We made out a lot throughout and eventually had sex, which is the big no-no. We kept that to ourselves. The only person on my side who knew was Ariel, my best friend. Ariel at this point was no longer in the religion. We became a couple and fell deeply in love and then this is when things went left. We got reckless and someone saw us together while out. They snitched to the elders. We were reprimanded for not letting them know about our relationship and coming close to sinning. Little did they know. Then they brought up the fact that I was not baptized.

Jason and I still stayed together but this time we let it be known to the rest of the congregations and whoever gossiped to others. We got side eyes. I especially got looked down on. I got told what I was doing was wrong by my own family. Getting told to be baptized would solve the problem and we could get married. Jason proposed to me a few months later and I said yes. After this happened, he started to change. He became verbally abusive and started pressuring me about baptism because it was making him look bad. I even told him about my strained relationship with my father while he was alive, and he used that to attack me. He would mention how my father saw I was a bad seed, and I can't do anything right. He was making feel undeserving of love. I was heading towards depression but was always good at hiding it in front of people.

We were at a gathering and I felt like I did not want to be there as people were expressing their opinions wordlessly. He told me to smile and be happy, and when I didn't he made a scene and said, "I don't know what made me want to propose to you. You won't get baptized. You wanted sex before marriage. I should have dumped you a while ago." The look on my face was of shock and anger along with hurt. I saw everyone's faces, including my family. I looked at him and said, "I can't believe you turned on me like this! Acting like you're so innocent. I can't believe I fell in love with you! I don't know this..... this boy in front of me! Here's your stupid ring." I threw it at him, thankful that I had brought my car. I ran out and drove off in tears. I knew it was only an amount of time before everyone in the various congregations would find out. Gossip runs wild in the church. I heard my mom calling me but I could not face her or my sister, so I went to my best friend's house and told her everything. We drank and I stayed the night.

I woke up to so many messages. I dreaded the call to my mom. I called and we talked. Surprisingly she was understanding and did not agree with his behavior. We talked and she let me know whatever I decide to do she would always love me. My sister and brother, on the other hand, believed that though Jason's behavior was wrong, I still needed to be active in the religion and I shouldn't have been dating him anyway. I hung up. Throughout the week, people in the religion looked and shown their true feelings and I knew at this point I was done with the religion. Since I been in Chicago my whole life, I knew too many people and they were almost everywhere. I heard how he was spreading rumors about me that I was the one who was verbally abusive. I knew that in order to move on with my life I needed a new environment.

* * *

"I will stay at the apartments until you come out. I miss you and I was wrong." I came back to the present and knew he meant it. I could not go out. I called Zain.

"Hey, my beautiful queen."

"Hey, babe…" I was fighting tears. He fell silent. I knew he realized something was wrong.

"What's wrong? I hear it in your voice." I started crying and I fell to my knees.

"What happened, babe? Why are crying? Are you hurt? Where are you?"

"Babe… please come get me… I'm at home… my past is at the door… he is here… my ex-fiancé from Chicago… he found me and he won't leave." Jason knocked again, harder this time.

"Babe I'm on my way," Zain said. "Pack some things. You and Brownie are staying with me. You can stay on the phone with me until I get there."

"OK, please hurry."

"I will, and he better be gone by the time I get there. I can tell whatever he did it was serious, and he is going to feel pain."

"I'll start packing." As I got my suitcases I heard Jason knocking a few more times. Then it went quiet.

A while later, Zain said,

"OK, good I'm pulling up now. I don't see anyone so hopefully, he is gone. I'm coming up."

I opened the door for Zain and closed it behind him. He took me in his arms and saw the fear and dried tears in my eyes. He caressed my face and kissed me. We didn't say anything. He got my suitcase and I got Brownie, and we entered his car and put everything in. Zain was on the other side of the car putting Brownie inside, and I was about to get in when I felt someone grab my arm. It was Jason.

"Please don't run. I miss you. I messed up. Let me talk to you," he said.

I yanked my arm away as Zain came around. He grabbed Jason and punched him directly in the face. Jason fell and was struggling to get back up when Zain kicked him. Zain grabbed Jason by the shoulders and told him, "Don't you ever come near my girlfriend again because next time I won't let you live." He punched him in the face again. I saw Zain's face full of rage. He got up and turned to me and in a softened voice told me to get into the car. He climbed in too and we left. Through the rear-view mirror I watched Jason trying to get up but falling repeatedly.

We did not say anything for the whole ride. We reach his place and after we got in, I just sat on the couch. Numb. Zain came over and kneeled in front of me. He had a worried look on his face. He moved my hair out of my face. I shook myself back to reality.

"I'm sorry for getting you into this. I just needed to get out..."

"Don't ever say sorry, love. I'm your man. You are supposed to call me first. I'm here for you and I will protect you." I started tearing up again. Zain wiped my eyes and kissed me. I wiped my arms around his neck.

"I love you," I said.

"I love you too, baby." He held me.

After I calmed down I told him everything that happened and why I left Chicago. He understood. He made it clear that Jason did not deserve me and he was glad he punched him. We just lay on the couch for a while until I fell asleep. I woke up to him cooking. I got up and put my arms around him from behind and rested my head on his back. He put the spoon down and rubbed my hand and then turned around to hug me and kiss me.

"Thank you for everything," I said. I kissed him back and put all of my emotions into that kiss. I felt him holding me tighter and kissing me back.

He broke off the kiss to say, "Whew, babe, before you get me going let me finish."

I nodded, and as I went to sit down he slapped my ass. I smiled. I looked at my phone and saw missed calls from a mystery number. There were several texts from Jason, saying he deserved what happened but still wanted to talk to me. I did not want to get Zain going as I remembered his threat. I just deleted everything and blocked Jason.

After dinner, Zain and I cuddled and watched a movie. I wanted to show appreciation for what he did, so I got off the couch, got on my knees and took off his boxers. I took his dick in my hands massaged his balls and kissed them and then kissed the bottom half and the top half to the tip. I took his dick in my mouth and licked the head. He moaned. I started sucking on his dick while licking and he closed his eyes, "Shit baby just like that." I went to his spot and he grunted. I sucked and licked and he moaned and after a little bit, he came. After, I got up I said, "I just wanted to thank you." He got up and took me to bed.

He took off my clothes and he ran his hands all over my body. He kissed me from my forehead to my pussy. He caressed my breasts and licked them both and lightly bit my nipples. He kissed and sucked the spot on my neck which got me moaning. He spread my legs and while still on my spot he took his thumb and made a circular motion on my clit. I had a hard time being still. He then put the tip of his dick in me and pulled out and then back in and slowly entered me. Each stroke was slow. He started kissing me while going in and out. He looked at me and said, "I love you, Kelly, I hope you know this." I smiled and kissed him and sucked on his bottom lip. "I love you too, Zain". He was making love to me. He was slower, as if savoring every movement. He went from my lips, neck, and breast. He was feeling every part of me. I kissed his chest and neck and then his lips. He began to increase speed and I wrapped my legs around him as he pounded harder. I moaned and I dug my nails in his back as I got closer. He moaned and got up a little and put his hand on the headboard and he grunted more. He was going faster and had me bouncing.

"I'm about to cum! Shit!" He kept going and I came and then he did. He stayed in me for a minute and released his hand from the headboard and kissed me. We soon fell asleep. I was in his arms and felt safe.

The rest of the weekend was chilled. I called off work Monday for the first time since being at the firm, but I did some work from my laptop. I was still at Zain's, I took the dog out for a walk. After I put on sexy lingerie and put on his dress coat. Thank goodness for my shortness and his six-foot built. I was able to put it on cover everything. I called him and asked what he was up to. He was in his office at the restaurant. I let him know I was thinking of him before letting him get back to work. I was glad he had another vehicle since mine was still at the apartment. I got the keys and went to surprise him when the evening started. I reached the restaurant where, at this point, some of the employees knew me. I went to his office and found him at his desk.

"Hey love," I said.

"Hey babe."

"I just wanted to come and surprise you." I closed and locked the door.

"I'm glad you did. I'm close to finishing everything here."

I kissed him.

"Is this my coat?" I smiled and nodded. I then untied the knot and unbuttoned the coat and gave him a visual of my lavender lingerie. His eyes opened wide. I put my knee between his legs on the chair and kissed him and then his neck. He then put his arms in his coat and around me. He kissed me back and then to my neck. He took one hand and pushed his stuff to the side. He got up and took the coat off me. He laid me on the desk and took off my underwear and kissed my pussy and started licking and sucking. I tried not to make much noise since people were outside. I covered my mouth and muffled my moans; he did not stop but kept going until I came. It was hard to be quiet. Then he flipped me and had me leaning against the desk. He unbuckled his pants and let them drop. He took out his dick and entered me and he was going in and out, pumping me hard and fast. I heard him grunt softly while our flesh slapped against each other. He had one hand on my hair and was pulling while his other hand was on my ass rubbing and slapping it lightly in an effort to be quiet. He went faster and harder, and we came at the same time. He leaned on me for a minute before pulling out. We put our clothes back on and kissed each other, I asked him if I looked OK to go out. He helped me with my hair.

"See you back home," I said.

"I'll be there soon, love." We both smiled and I left. I put on a nonchalant face. I saw a couple of employees looking at me and I smirked. I wasn't sure if they heard but I was not going to ask. I left and returned to the condo.

Zain arrived not too long after I cooked dinner. Afterwards he gave me another gift. This time it was a diamond necklace. I told him he didn't have to but of course he let me know it would continue. We made love that night. I spent a few more nights at his place before returning to my apartment on the Saturday. Zain came with me and made sure I was good before he left. My girls were coming and we were going to dinner that night.

18

CHAPTER 18

While at dinner with the girls I told them all the details of the incident with Jason and Zain.

"Well, Zain is gaining more points in my book. You choose the right one," said Lena.

"I agree. At least you found someone who deserves you," Angela added.

"Yeah, I feel that way too. But enough about me. How are things between you and your men?"

Angela went first.

"Kevin is great. We have a great connection and he is planning for me to meet his family soon."

"Yassss! You know what's coming next," I said.

"Uh huh, we will be hearing some news soon. I can feel it," said Lena.

Angela chuckled.

"We will see. How about you, Lena?"

"Things are really good with Christian. Surprisingly. He respects what I do and actually seems to care but you guys know I'm cautious."

"We know, but at least it sounds like you're giving him a chance," I said.

After dinner we went home. I spent the rest of the weekend doing a self-care day and preparing for the week ahead.

<u>A month later.....</u>

I was at the gym with my girls after work. Zain called, asking where I was so that he could drop off a couple of law books I'd left at his place and desperately needed. He let me know he would come to the gym. I told him to let me know when he arrived and I would meet him outside. I did not want him to come in as I saw Kyle earlier. Kyle had been giving me looks but left me alone. We had just finished the workout and were heading to the locker rooms when Zain let me know he had arrived and had come inside. When I told my girls he was in the gym they told me to hurry up and go. I saw him at the front and kissed him.

"Hey, love here are your books."

"Thanks, babe, I appreciate you bringing them."

"Where are Lena and Angela?"

"They went ahead to the locker rooms. We just finished."

"OK, babe. I will call you...." He stopped talking. I followed his eyes and saw that he was looking at Kyle. *Oh shit. This can't be happening.*

"Babe, what was—"

"—What is he doing here?" I turned back and acknowledged Kyle's presence.

"He works here."

"What the fuck? Are you *serious*? You never said anything about that. Why do you even come to this gym? There are others."

"Babe, please don't cause a scene. I come to this one because it's close to my office and I had a deal too."

"Are you still seeing him?"

"You can't be serious! Of course not. I'm with you and only you. So please calm down."

"Do you still talk to him?"

"No, I don't. He is not my trainer anymore." *Shit, why did I say that?* Zain looked at me with so much anger and hurt.

"Trainer? Wow, he's been your trainer all this time."

"Before we got together, babe. I have stopped that..."

"Is everything alright?" I turned around and it was Kyle. *Why did he even come over? He'll just make things worse.*

"Go away Kyle, stay out of this," I said.

"Wow, really Kelly? It seems like he's still in your life."

"No, he is not! I'm with you. Why can't you believe me? I never gave you a reason to doubt me so why now?"

"Yeah man, she is loyal. She slapped me for kissing her when I came by that day," said Kyle.

"Go away Kyle," I told him. "I said leave me alone."

"I'm going, I just wanted to make sure you good."

"Kelly, I can't talk to you right now," Zain said. "I need to go." I grabbed his arm.

"Zain, please just listen to me. There is nothing going on."

"Let go of my arm Kelly. I need to leave before I punch him."
I let go.

"Kelly, please don't call me. I can't do this right now," said
Zain. He walked out. I looked at Kyle and felt like punching him
myself. I was so angry that tears ran down my face. I walked past
him and went to the locker room. Angela and Lena saw my red
eyes and tears.

"What happened Kelly?" Lena asked.

"Zain saw Kyle and accused me of seeing Kyle behind his
back. I told him I wasn't, but my stupid self mentioned that he
was my trainer though not anymore. Then Kyle must have seen
us arguing. He came over and made things worse. Zain walked
off and told me he can't talk to me right now and that I should
leave him alone."

"What the hell?! Zain should have given you chance to really
explain. I'm sorry Kelly," said Angela. They gave me a hug. They
waited until I calmed down and then headed home.

I sent one text message to Zain:

*Hey babe. I just want to make it clear. I have not been seeing him
behind your back. I have not been talking to him. I'm with you and
been loyal to you. I love you and I hope you know that and believe
me.*

I did not get a reply. I cried myself to sleep that night.

The week went on I still hadn't not heard from Zain. At this
point I was wondering whether he even wanted me anymore. It
was hurting. Friday came and I was in the office burying myself
in work. All of a sudden I heard shouting and screaming. I went

outside and heard more shouting from a man towards the front of the building. Rochelle and I looked at each other, then Miguel came out. The other attorneys and staff all came out. We saw a man, who was clearly furious, walk from around the corner, pull out a gun and start shooting. Everyone started running. People were screaming and pushing people. Someone pushed me and I fell onto Miguel. I tried to get up quickly, as did Miguel. The man saw us and aimed the gun at me. He pulled the trigger and Miguel jumped in front of me. The shooter continued to walk, made another turn and began shooting in a different direction. Then he went out of sight.

"Miguel! Are you alright? Please be alright." He grunted in pain and was covered in blood. It looked like the bullet hit his shoulder. I got up and pulled him into a supply closet nearby. I closed it. The blood was pouring out and I knew I needed to slow down the bleeding. I took off my jacket, put it on his wound and called 911. Miguel kept grunting and was in a lot of pain. I held my jacket in place.

"Why did you jump in front of me?"

"Why...why wouldn't I? I know I'm cocky but not evil. Plus...you got to... know that... I like you... a lot."

"No, you don't Miguel."

"You... don't realize how... beautiful you are, inside and out."

"We can talk about this later when we get out of this." We stayed put and heard shots here and there. After a while a silence. All of a sudden we heard a bunch of footsteps. Then voices over a walkie-talkie, like it was the police. I heard a knock on the door and we were silent.

"This is the SWAT. Is anyone in there?"

"Yes, there's two of us."

"I'm officer Thompson. You can open the door slowly." I opened the door and there were two officers pointing guns at us.

"He's injured," I told them. "He needs medical attention." I got up with my hands up. Two of the team carried Miguel and a third guided us to the exit. When we got outside, we were directed to medical. There was a crowd behind the tape. Rochelle made it out of the building and we gave each other a hug. The medical team checked me and prepared to take Miguel to the hospital.

"KELLY! KELLY!" I heard my name and knew it was Zain's voice. I looked and saw him behind the tape. He was trying to get past but the police would not let him. I heard him say, "That is my girlfriend right there. I need to know if she is OK. Please let me go to her." I told Miguel I'd be right back. I ran to Zain and the police saw me coming. "Kelly!" "Zain!" I went under the rope and Zain grabbed me in his arms and kissed me with so much intensity. He held me tight. "Baby, I'm sorry for everything. I should have believed you from the start. I love you. Are you ok?" He looked me over and saw the blood. "Where are you hurt?"

"I'm OK, thanks to my colleague. He jumped in front of me and took the bullet. He got shot in the shoulder. It's his blood. I used my jacket to slow down the blood flow. I should go check on him. I have to thank him."

A police officer came up and wanted to talk to me. I went to follow the officer.

Zain said, "I won't leave you. I will be right here when you are done, babe." I nodded. I saw the ambulance leave and I gave my version of what happened. The SWAT team found the guy but had to kill him. Apparently, it was a disgruntled client. After I was allowed to leave, I went to Zain and I saw Kyle in the crowd. He looked at me and I could tell he wanted to come to me but when he saw Zain he just nodded at me and left. Zain took me in his arms and kissed me again, asking if we could go to the hospital. Zain agreed and we walked to his car. He asked me what happened before we left and I told him.

At the hospital, Miguel was already in recovery. When I got permission to see him, Zain waited outside. Miguel was awake and resting.

"Hey Kelly, you did not have to come and see me."

"Of course, I did. You were there for me and I'm the reason why you are in here."

"I just want to add 'hero' to the list of things that is great about me."

I rolled my eyes and laughed.

"Well, I wanted to say thank you and I will never forget this." I squeezed his hand lightly.

"I would do it again." He looked at me with a more serious expression and squeezed my hand back. He then rubbed his thumb across my hand. I did not know how to respond and froze for a second.

"I meant what I said. I really like you and I know you are with someone and I can't do anything about it. But after what happened I needed to say it."

"I really don't understand it. I continue to be surprised how I even pull very attractive guys in general."

"So, you think I'm attractive?" He smiled. I shook my head and chuckled.

"You just admitted it and also why do you think that way?"

"Let's not focus on me. You're the injured one and what is important is you getting better."

"I really want to know, though. You know I ask questions."

I sighed.

"Yes, you do." We laughed. "Well, it's just I know I'm not skinny and don't have the perfect body guys drool over. I dealt with this my whole life. I have always been the invisible one growing up."

"You are attractive. Curvy and all. You are not going to believe what I'm about to say but the guys who are like that are limited thinkers and just have egos issues."

"Wow, who knew you thought that deep."

"I know, right?"

"See, now you messed up." We laughed.

"I'm glad you'll be OK. I better go and let you rest."

"Thanks for coming to see me. I hope you come back too."

"Will do."

I walked out and found Zain sitting.

"How is he doing?" Zain asked.

"He will be OK. I'm ready to get out of these clothes."

"OK babe, just hold on one second." He left and went into Miguel's room. I have to admit, I was a little nervous about the conversation they would have.

A few minutes later he came out.

"I just wanted to thank him myself for taking the bullet. I don't know how I would have been if anything happened to you."

I kissed him and then he took me home. I got calls from my girls and let them know I was OK. Zain asked if he could stay over or if I wanted to stay at his place. He said he didn't want to sleep without me tonight and, honestly, I did not want to be alone either. I went to my place since we were there. I took a shower and changed into comfortable clothes. I was numb. He ordered some food. We ate and got into bed. When I lay down, the tears came out uncontrollably. All my emotions came all at once. I cried out and Zain took me in his arms and held me. He told me to let it all out. I grabbed onto his arms tightly and leaned on him. I could only hear him say, "I know babe. Let it out. I'm here. Hold on to me." I cried myself to sleep.

19

CHAPTER 19

The next day, Zain woke me up to breakfast in bed. I ate and returned several phone calls. Internally I was a mess but I did not want a repeat of the night before. The office itself would be closed for the next week so I would be working from home. Zain had to go to his office, while I visited Miguel in the hospital. I brought him a get-well card and some balloons. I knew I would never be able to thank him enough.

"Hey, Miguel!"

"Hey, Kelly. How are you?"

"I should be the one asking you that, but I'm ok."

"I'm good. They've been giving me the good stuff." We laughed.

"I want to say thank you again for what you did. I will never be able to repay you." I put his card down and tied the ballon to his bed.

"You're welcome, and there is no need. You're worth it."

I blushed.

"Have you had a lot of visitors?"

"Not a lot, except my parents and my sister. They were driving me crazy."

"That's to be expected. Families worry."

"I'm sure you know your boyfriend came and saw me after you walked out."

"Yeah, he said he wanted to thank you."

"Yeah, he did...." Miguel looked off to the side with slight anger on his face.

"What is it? Did something else happen?"

"It's nothing."

"Spill it." He shook his head.

"Fine, then I'll just leave."

"OK, OK. He thanked me for taking the bullet. He also... asked what made me do it."

"Oh... what did you say?"

"I told him I considered you as a friend and as a man I felt had to. I would feel bad if I did not do anything. He took the answer but I don't think he fully believed me. I kind of didn't want him to." I was silent for a second.

"Why didn't you?"

"Because I wanted him to know I could be a threat. I know you love him. I saw how you reacted when you heard him call you. I want him to know I like you because if he hurts you... I would take my shot." I was shocked and blushing. "If this has taught me anything, it taught me to not wait if I don't have to."

"I'm not that special."

"Yes, you are. I know I act arrogant but I feel I have to be in this career. I know you are a good person and good at your job. We go back and forth talking shit. I just see how intelligent you are and while you're already attractive you make yourself even more attractive when we talk."

"That was really sweet and thank you. You're really good at your job too and obviously really attractive. You must date model types and I'm not a model type, as you can see."

"You don't know what I like. I like meat on my women. Also, I know there are plus-size models out there. I wish I could take you out so you could get to know the real me outside of the office, but I will respect your relationship."

"I thank you for that and I don't feel like going to HR either." We laughed.

"How are you really, though, with everything that happened?" I asked with a serious tone.

"I'm OK. I do remember everything and it has been replaying in my mind without trying to. How about you?"

I looked down. A tear escaped my eye.

"I've been reliving it too. I kinda broke down last night after I got in bed. Zain had to hold me."

Miguel took my hand and held it. I let him. We shared something that we would have to live with. We talked some more, but eventually I knew it was time to go.

"Well, I will get going so you can continue to rest. I'll talk to you later."

"I'm glad you came to see me. Thank you."

"You're welcome. It's the least I could do." I gave Miguel a light hug. "You know we can be friends at least," I said.

"I know." He smiled a little. I walked to the door.

"Hey, Kelly?" I turned. "I just want to know one thing." I nodded. "With what you know now about how I feel and if you were single... would you go out with me?"

I paused and thought about it.

"Yeah, I mean you're kinda cute." We chuckled.

"Glad to hear it."

I left the hospital and ran some errands. I never tried to look at Miguel in that way but after all, what happened, a part of me wondered. But in the end, I was happy with my relationship. I'm a Leo at heart. I met up with my girls at the gym as I needed a distraction. As we were on the treadmill, I saw Kyle heading in my direction. I glanced at my girls. Kyle came up and said, "Hey Kelly, I just wanted to ask how you were doing since everything happened. I'm glad you're OK."

"I'll be OK. Thanks for asking."

"Good. I know you don't need it but if you do need anything you know my number."

"Thanks, Kyle."

I watched him walk away.

"That was kind of awkward but sweet," said Lena.

"Yeah, it was," I said. We continued with our workout.

When I got back home, I walked in and I could hear some Maxwell playing. Candles were lit everywhere. Zain emerged from the bedroom and held me in his arms.

"Welcome home love". He kissed me, put my bag down, then took my hand and guided me to the dining table. He had cooked dinner. Afterwards, he ran a bath for me. I could not help but feel loved. Then he took me to the room, and we made love. He eventually laid me down with me and wrapped his arm around me and was just looking at me. "I'm so happy you're OK. When my employees told me what happened and I realized it was your firm, everything became a blur and I just knew I needed to get to you. I had to know if you were OK. I don't want to lose you." He kissed me again and I kissed him back.

"Kelly?"

"Yes, love?"

"I want to ask you something but I'm pretty sure you won't like it."

"What is it?" I had a concerned look on my face and already had several scenarios in my head.

"Well, just to start off I can see a future with you and after what happened I don't want that to ever happened again because I don't want to think of a future without you. What I'm asking is, would you stop being an attorney if we were to get married?"

"What?! I love being an attorney. I worked so hard for this in spite of limited support. I can't give it up."

"You wouldn't have to work. I would take care of you. I don't want to think of another crazy person to come and do the same thing and find out you were hurt or worse."

"You're asking me to sacrifice a big part of who I'm. I can't do that."

"I know I'm asking a lot but please consider it."

"And if I don't, then what? You would just let our relationship end?" He did not respond; he just looked at the ground.

"We are not even engaged and you're asking me this. I can't

even do this right now." I got out of bed and put my robe on. Zain he got out too. He came to me but I backed away. He had an *I-fucked-up look on his face* as he put on his clothes.

"I'll go back to my place but, please, at least think about it. I care about you and I love you." Zain walked out. I ended up pacing for a little bit, pissed off at what Zain was asking of me. This was more than a compromise. He texted me a little later, asking me to reach out when I was ready. I rolled my eyes. I got in bed so I could sleep. Another text came in from Miguel.

Hey Kelly, I just wanted to let you know I will be released tomorrow. Just to tell you in case you were going to come by again. If you want to check on me again you can come through my place anytime. As friends of course, but like I said, if he messes up, I'm ready.

I was still in shock about Miguel and realized there was obviously a different side to him. His smile and the look of compassion in his eyes. The romantic thoughts in my head scared me a little as I knew I wasn't single. I tried to shake him out of my mind but then Kyle came to mind. The way he looked concerned for me. And no matter how much I tried to push him away he always seemed to come. How did I even get here? Me a plus-size woman who was overlooked when growing up somehow pulled three very sexy men. I was starting to get confused. I know I have pulled other sexy men but nothing like this.

I loved Zain but for me to end a career that I put my all in is something I will never do. He was there for me and did not judge my past. He spoiled me without even asking. He was sweet to me and understood what I'd been through. He loved me.

Kyle had also been there for me. He was still a mystery. I didn't know if I could trust him. He was persistent.... very persistent. I didn't like the fact that he ghosted me either. Even after everything that happened, he did make sure I was OK. That was sweet of him.

Then there was Miguel. The one who came from left field. As much as we went back and forth talking shit, I was ashamed to admit I liked it. There were several reasons as to why it should be a no for him. One is that we worked together. Second, he could be very arrogant but maybe not as much since I met a different side of him. Third, I didn't understand him. He took a bullet for me, though. That impacted me so much. The way he told me how he felt yet he respected my relationship.

My mind was going in different directions. I needed to stop thinking. I just scrolled through social media and went to sleep. I woke up to a few texts, checked my group chats with my girls and I nearly screamed. I quickly called Lena.

"Hello?"

"OH MY GOD!!!!" I screamed. "CONGRATULATIONS!!!!!!! I'M SO HAPPY FOR YOU!! You got to tell me how he proposed to you and don't leave anything out!"

Lena chuckled. She mentioned how Christian took her to her favorite restaurant and proposed after dinner. I made it clear we needed to celebrate. Lena agreed.

"We can make a couple of dates."

"Ummm, yea."

"What is it, Kelly? What happened? Are we going to have to hurt Zain?"

"I don't want to discuss him. We are going to celebrate you and Christian."

"Nope, you are not going to avoid the topic."

"Fine. Me and Zain had a fight."

"About what?"

"After everything that happened at the office, he says he sees a future together but would like for me to quit being an attorney if we are to get married."

"No way! He got some nerve. Ugh! I wish Christian would say something like that to me."

"This happened last night and we have not talked yet."

"I'm sorry. You're not going to quit, right?"

"No, I told him I worked too hard to get to where I'm."

"Good! Did you guys break up?"

"As of right now...no, but we'll see."

"Ugh, he had to go and fuck up. We were all rooting for him."

"Yeah... side note... something else happened."

"What?!"

"Remember, I told you about the guy who took the bullet for me?"

"Yes."

"Well, he kinda confessed he really likes me."

"Oh my god. Look at you girl! Well, if you and Zain do break up that guy can take his place. He did take a bullet."

I chuckled.

"We will see."

The girls and I planned to have a celebratory dinner the following weekend. Lena suggested if Zain couldn't come then I should bring Miguel. I didn't know what would happen to me and Zain. In the meantime, I decided to make a get-well cake for Miguel. I felt obligated to do all I could for him. I really didn't know how to thank him. I made the cake and had Miguel text me his address. Then I texted Zain and asked if we could talk later in the evening. Zain agreed.

20

CHAPTER 20

I went to see Miguel but got lost along the way and had to call him. He guided me and I made it. He greeted me at the door, giving me a hug with his good arm. He smelled good. I gave him his cake.

"So, not only are good at your job and beautiful, you can also bake. Now I'm really going to steal you from your boyfriend." I shook my head chuckled, then thought about Zain. It must have shown on my face because when I came back to reality Miguel was looking at me confusedly.

"I hope you like chocolate," I said.

"No, we are not going to ignore what just happened. What's up?"

"It's nothing." Miguel just stared at me like he knew it was a lie.

"Damn, were you studying me?"

142

"I'm an attorney too."

"Ugh, fine. Me and my boyfriend had an argument."

"Huh, are you guys still together?" He had the look of anticipation.

I rolled my eyes.

"Yes, we are still together... for now," I mumbled.

"You know I ask questions. What happened?"

"That is between us... but I do want to ask you a question as a guy."

"Shoot."

"After what happened in the office, do you still want to be an attorney?"

"Yes. And please don't tell me you want to quit."

"No, I still want to be an attorney. If someone who you loved was also an attorney in another firm and the shooting happened to them, would you ask them to give up their profession?"

"I would not ask them to stop. I would worry for a while but I wouldn't do that to them. Too much work goes into becoming an attorney."

"That's good of you."

"So, I take it your guy asked to stop being one?"

I remained silent.

"Got it," Miguel said. "Well, he should not have asked you that. That is not his choice to make."

"Yeah, that's what I said."

"Oooh, I'm good. Already got him messing up," Miguel chuckled. I just smiled and shook my head.

"Well, if you guys do break up, call me and I will show up." I just looked at him with disbelief.

"I'm not playing, mami." He had a serious look on his face.

"Umm, OK." When he said that, I was ashamed of the feeling I had below my waist.

We talked for a little more and then I left. I went home first and got cute so Zain could see what he was jeopardizing. Then I went to his place. I knocked on the door, and when he answered he only had on sweat pants. *Damn, he did this on purpose.* I kept my composure and said, "Hey." He let me in and I sat on the couch.

He sat next to me but I refused to look at him directly. He took my hand and held it.

"Look, I know I don't have a right to ask that of you but I'm just worried about that ever happening again. I want you in my life."

"I really appreciate you caring about me, but you are right about one thing. You don't have the right to ask me to quit. I will not quit."

"Babe, please! Say we get married and have kids. I don't want to have to explain to our kids why their mother is not coming home."

"I hear you but you do realize even just stepping outside there is a possibility of something happening but we don't stay inside because of it."

"You really went lawyer on me just now."

"It's just my view and plus as I mentioned before, I worked too hard for this. I'm close to junior partner and I don't want to lose that." Zain looked at me for a second without saying anything.

"Zain, do you want to break up?" He looked down and then back at me but no words came out.

"Got it."

I felt tears in my eyes. I got up and started heading towards the door. I felt Zain grab my arm and turned me back around and took me in his arms and kissed me. I wanted to fight him but I couldn't. I kissed him back and started making out. I felt on his arms. He felt on be back with one hand, holding me close to him. His other hand was on my face while we continued to kiss. He then picked me up by my legs and sat me on the counter. He never took his lips off of mine. He then lifted up my dress and started rubbing on my thighs. He went to my spot on my neck and started licking. I knew this was not the time for this but he was turning me on too much. He started rubbing my nipples. I let out a moan. He continued to kiss me while he pulled off my underwear. He pulled down his pants and I felt his tip on the outer lips of my pussy. He slowly put it in and made sure to fill me with his whole dick. He started grinding on me. He went in and out. He started picking up pace. He looked at me with a pleading look and then kissed me with so much eagerness. He felt so good and he started pounding me while still kissing and playing with my nipple. We came fast. We were trying to catch our breath. Then looked at each other. I was waiting for him to tell me that the whole idea was stupid and we should stay together but not a word. I got off the counter and said, "Nothing?"

He just looked at me and said, "Please."

"I guess we are breaking up," I said. Tears rolled down my face.

Zain said, "I don't want us to but I don't want to have to worry every day if something will happen."

I turned and walked out. I heard him say he was sorry but that didn't mean anything. I drove home in a daze and went to bed.

I woke up the next day to a couple of texts. One from Zain and one from Miguel.

Zain:

Hey love, I just want you to know I won't ever stop loving you. I hope you reconsider.

I did not respond.

Miguel:

Hey, just checking on you. Did you have the talk with your boyfriend?

I was not sure if I wanted to tell Miguel what happened. I thought about it for a few minutes and then....

Hey Miguel, who says you deserve to know. I see you are being your normal nosey self. Lol. Well, yes, I did have a conversation with him.

I left it on that note on purpose. I went on with my day did some work. I enjoyed working from home. It did not take long to get a response from Miguel.

Are available or not?

If I were, who says I would go out with you?

Come on Kelly, you said you would at the hospital.

Yeah, I said it but maybe I was just trying to help with your recovery. Lol

Ouch, I guess not

Ok ok, I had my fun. Yeah I guess I'm single now.

Oh really...well how about we go on a date.

Lol, I just got out of a relationship. I don't know if I want or should go on a date right now.

I get it but how about we just go out to dinner to get to know each other and to celebrate my recovery

He got me there.

Fine, we can go out but there is a price.

O...what is it?

My friend just got in engaged and there is a celebratory dinner this weekend. Would you go with me as my date?

Scratch that... as my friend.

Yeah, I'm cool with that. We can go on our date the next day.

Ok, that would work.

I'll message Lena and let her know everything. She was happy I would still have a date.

I mean a friend to bring

Right, it's a date.

Friday night came and it was the celebratory dinner for Lena and her fiancé. I already talked with Miguel earlier and his shoulder was pretty much back to normal. He insisted on picking me up. I got ready and wore a blue v-neck dress with a gold belt. I straightened my hair. After I finished my makeup, I heard a knock and saw it was Miguel. His brown eyes grew wide and he opened his mouth but nothing came out. I smiled and said hi. After he snapped out of it he returned the greeting.

"You look beautiful, Kelly."

"Thanks, Miguel, you look very handsome yourself." Miguel had on a nice blue suit with no tie and a slightly opened button shirt.

"I mean you've always been beautiful but I've never seen you dressed up like this."

"Thanks... I think."

"No... I mean..."

I chuckled.

"It's OK, Miguel. I get what you mean." This was a different side of him that I had not known was there. I found it really attractive.

"OK, good. Are you ready?" I nodded and grabbed my purse and jacket. The car ride there was not too bad. We discussed work but Miguel then put on some music and told me more about his recovery, physically and mentally. He even asked how I was doing. I let him know that I was taking it day by day, with each day better than the one before. He took my hand and squeezed it. This gave me a tingling feeling and made me continue seeing Miguel in a different light. I was witnessing a more tender side to him.

We reached the restaurant where we found Lena and the rest of the party. Lena and Angela were looking over Miguel and then looked at me and smiled approvingly. I gave the happy couple hugs, and then hugged the rest of the people I knew. I introduced Miguel to everyone. We sat and started talking with everyone and Miguel decided to put his arm over the top of my chair. He decided to get closer and I could smell his cologne more. He smelled good. Miguel seemed to fit right in and was charming everyone.

Then Lena's fiancé burst out saying, "Hey Zain! Glad you could make it."

I almost choked on my wine. Lena mouthed that she didn't know. She nudge her fiancé side. He looked at her and said "What?" and then both of them looked at me. He apologized and said Zain was his friend too. I turned and saw Zain walking up to the tables. He looked at me with a sad expression but then saw Miguel and a little anger appeared. He hugged the couple then sat a couple of seats away from Miguel and me. He did not make eye contact with me. *This is very awkward.* I turned to look at Miguel. He had a big stupid grin on his face. He was enjoying this and even scooted closer to me, wrapping his arms around me and whispering in my ear: "I know that dude wants to fight me but you are worth fighting for. It was his loss and my gain." I looked at Miguel in shock but felt kind of turned on.

Aside from Zain's awkward vibes, the evening proceeded peacefully, and we toasted the future bride and groom. As we all were getting ready to leave, Miguel went to the bathroom. Zain approached me and said, "Damn, you look beautiful. I miss you, Kelly." Just then, Miguel came over and put his arm around my waist and asked if I was ready. I nodded. As I turned around to leave, Zain reached for me but Miguel came between us and burst out saying, "She's safe with me. You fucked up your chance with her. Now let me treat her right." Zain angrily drew his face close to Miguel and said, "She deserves the world and you can't give that to her. She needs to be with me." I got mad at this point and felt his words come back to me. "You had me, Zain, and I wanted a future with you but you wanted to control what I do with my life." Zain looked at me with disappointment and walked out. Lena apologized over and over. I let her know I was not mad at her since she did not know. The drive home started on a quiet note until Miguel broke the silence.

"I'm sorry I said anything but I didn't want him to cause you any more pain. It was written on your face. I know that you're fresh out of a relationship and probably will want time but I'm here and ready whenever you are. I know we have a date tomorrow but if you wanted to wait, I understand."

I was silent for a moment thinking about what he said.

"Thanks for being there for me again. I really don't know what to say. I mean you have shown me a whole new side of you and it says a lot in a good way. Yes, I'm fresh out of the relationship and maybe I should slow things, but since we already planned for tomorrow, we can keep that and see where we go from there. Is that, OK?"

"That is more than OK. I would not want to disappoint you in any way. I really like you and don't want to fuck it up like that other guy did." I looked out the window in silence as my relationship with Zain flashed in my mind. I shook myself back to reality. We talked about everyone at the party, and Miguel had me laughing. We reached my apartment and he walked me to my door.

"Thanks for coming with my Miguel."

"No problem, I just hope your friends would approve of me."

I laughed.

"I'll know very soon."

"Well, good night Kelly." He came very close to me. I could feel his body heat. He gave me a hug and then kissed my cheek. He then looked into my eyes like he was trying to read my mind, then kissed me. I felt my body heat up and kissed him back. We started to make out as he wrapped his arms around me holding me tight against his body. I felt his tongue reaching for my tongue and I accepted it. He pressed his body against mine as I leaned against the door. "Damn baby, I want you in every way." I was so drawn in but Zain popped into my mind. Also, this was my work colleague. I woke myself out of this moment and stopped him. Miguel stopped and looked at me and said, "I'm sorry, I just couldn't help it. You are so beautiful and I been wanting to kiss you for so long now."

I blushed and let him know it was OK. I told Miguel goodnight and he let me know that he would call tomorrow about the date. After I closed the door Brownie greeted me and I petted him, but was still in a daze about everything that happened. Seeing Zain since we broke up. Seeing him getting angry because of Miguel's presence. Seeing a different side of Miguel outside of work. I was attracted to him even though a big part of me felt I shouldn't because we work together. I was confused and the date the following night could be more confusing. I was having second thoughts. I decided I would sleep on it. After taking a shower I played with myself, thinking of Miguel; I wanted him after what happened tonight. I went to bed, thinking of the next day.

21

CHAPTER 21

The next day I handled my responsibilities and spent time with Brownie. My girls and I ended up on a three-way call, talking about the previous night.

"I'm really happy you guys came yesterday. I still can't believe I'm engaged. Also, I'm so sorry Kelly for having Zain there. I didn't know Christian invited him," Lena said.

"It's OK, Lena. They did become friends and I should have known he would be there. I just wasn't ready for the confrontation," I said.

"Yeah, I saw from a distance and I felt awkward for all of y'all," Angela said.

"I'm just glad it did not end up in a fight, like it almost was with Zain and Kyle," I sighed.

"Yeah, you're right about that. Speaking of Kyle... I saw him and he asked about you," said Angela.

153

"Oh? And what was said?"

"He just asked how were you doing, and I told him you were good. He also asked how things were with Zain..."

"Why did you go quiet?"

"Well, you see what had happened was... he saw my facial expression because I rolled my eyes. Then he said, "So dude fucked up." I then looked away and he told me I didn't have to say anything. I'm so sorry but I didn't tell him."

I sighed.

"It's OK, Angela, I know it was not intentional. Also, I can't really think about him right now since I do have a date tonight with Miguel. That was the deal — if he came to the dinner then I would go on a date with him."

"How do you feel about Miguel?" Angela asked.

"I'm confused about him. Don't get me wrong – he is fine as hell!"

"Yes, he is," said Angela and Lena in unison. We all laughed.

"I'm confused because he is such a narcissist, or so I thought. It's like outside of work he is completely different. Like I couldn't stand him, but now I'm kind of drawn to him. Also, the fact the man took a bullet for me, and him claiming to want me after. I can't ignore that."

"Well, you owe it to yourself to see where it goes," said Angela.

"Yeah, but the main issue is that he is my colleague. I know eventually if we keep going we will have to let HR know."

"That's understandable. See if it's worth it first," said Lena.

"Will do."

We talked more about last night and the upcoming wedding. When we got off the call I got ready for the date. Miguel had texted earlier in the day to confirm whether I was still down for the date. I told him I was. He told me we were going to do axe throwing then eat out afterwards. I was excited as I heard so much about it and seen videos on social media. When Miguel picked me up I could not help finding myself even more attracted to him. His smile was just... I can't describe.

"Hey sexy, you ready?" I nodded and closed the door. Miguel took my hand and we walked to the car. We talked and danced to music. We reached our destination and entered our axe throwing station. We got competitive with each other and I loved it. We were roasting one another and laughing throughout. Afterwards we ate at a steakhouse in a booth where we sat literally next to each other. I think Miguel planned that because he put his arm behind me. I could smell his cologne. It was nice as usual. We ended up feeding each other off our plates. I felt so comfortable around him.

"Wow, who knew this side of you existed, Miguel."

He laughed.

"I told you I was different outside of work. I have to play the role to succeed."

"Yeah, I can understand that. Being a person of color, we have no choice."

He nodded.

"You are so beautiful, Kelly. I'm happy you are here with me."

"I'm glad I'm here too. But there is one thing we have to talk about and that is the firm."

"What you mean?"

"I mean, if we continue this you know we are going to have to go to HR."

"Yeah, I know but we can worry about that later."

He dropped me off after dinner. At my door he wrapped his arms around my waist and pulled me against him and kissed me. I felt shockwaves throughout my body. A part of me felt like I shouldn't be doing this but it felt so good. I wrapped my arms around his shoulders and was kissing back.. Miguel was now holding me tight and our breathing got faster. I didn't care about anything else. We entered the apartment while still making out. We started taking off our clothes and made it to my bedroom I leaned back on the bed as I only had my underwear and bra on at this point. He followed and he only had his boxers on. He was ripped as I thought he would be. I felt intoxicated by his kisses and as he got on top of me and he started kissing and lightly sucking on my neck. I let out a low moan. He pulled down my bra and took my breast in his mouth and flicked his tongue on my nipple and lightly pinching my other nipple. He made eye contact with me and I was being turned on even more. I felt myself getting wetter. "Be mine Kelly," said Miguel as he switched to my other breast. I arched myself to him and letting out soft moans. My hand found its way to the back of his head and stroked it. "I always wanted you since I first met you." He then pulled off my panties, spread my thighs apart and kisses my pussy lips. He spread my pussy lips apart and licked my clit. I started moaning louder as I heard him moan softly. He started licking me more. I felt a couple of fingers go in and out and let out a loud moan. I heard him say, "Maldita sea, gime un poco más por mi bebé. (Damn, moan some more for me baby)". It turned me on even more than I would ever think it could with him speaking Spanish to me. I didn't know what he was saying but it sounded so sexy. His fingers found my spot and I started squirming. But just I felt myself get closer to an orgasm, Miguel freaking stopped! He sat up and chuckled and said, "No mami, not yet." I scrunched up my nose at him. "You don't realize how cute you are when you do that," he said. I blushed.

He pulled me down to the edge of the bed and he took off his boxers and saw his big dick up and ready. He saw me bite my lip and said, "Eres tan sexy y quiero que seas mia. ("You are so sexy and I want you to be mine"). He rubbed my pussy and kissed me on my lips, my neck, my chest and my stomach. He put the tip at my pussy and had it going up and down getting my juices on it. He looked at me and moaned. He put it in and I gasped and he grunted. He was going in and out, slowly. "¡Mierda!" He felt so good.

"Mmmm", I said.

Miguel leaned over and rubbed my breast and kissed me passionately. He started to go faster and he stood back up and held on to my thighs as he pounded me. We both started making noises. I sat up a little and he grabbed me and kissed me. He picked me up while still inside me and turned and sat on the edge of the bed with my legs on the bed. I leaned back a little while he was holding me around my waist with one arm. I started hopping on his dick and he was meeting me with each thrust. I started to yelp a little and he mumbled in Spanish. He put his hand on the side of my face and had me look at his sex face with my own sex face. He pulled my head to his and put my arms around him and we made out as we continue to thrust. I felt myself getting closer and I broke the kissing and my breathing increased more.

"You about to cum babe?"

"Yes! I'm... I'm getting close."

"So am I babe. Shit!"

"O Miguel don't stop. Fuck me!"

"I won't stop Kelly. I will give it to you all the time if you want. I always thought about taking you in the office and doing you on the table."

That sent me over. "I'm cumming!"

"Fuck, I'm cumming too."

We went faster and harder. I felt myself cumming and yelled and Miguel moaned loudly holding me tight and he was pushed his dick in me as far as he could so he put all his cum in me. I felt his dick throbbing inside.

After a few minutes, we were coming off our high. I was still sitting on him with his dick inside me. He kissed me deeply for a minute and then paused. He looked at me and moved my hair out of my face and smiled. I smiled back. I looked at him and then looked him over and saw the scarring from the wound on his shoulder. Sadness took me over a little as I gently stroked the scar. I guess my face showed how I was feeling because he took my hand and kissed my fingers. Then he looked into my eyes and said, "Hey, it's ok and I'm ok. Don't let that affect us right now. I'm here."

I felt tears developing and all the emotions of everything between us came to a head and I kissed him with all the passion I had. He held me tight, kissing me and caressing my face. Tears ran down my face and my eyes were closed, taking him all in. We will forever have this traumatic experience between us and how he protected me. I realized at this moment I was falling for him. We finally broke from kissing and I saw his tears. He wiped mine away and kissed my forehead. I wiped his away and kissed his nose. He lay me down in bed and asked if could he stay. I said yes. We slid under the covers and slept with my head on his chest.

The next morning, I Miguel still in bed but awake, looking at me.

"Good morning, sexy," he murmured, then kissed me.

"Good morning, handsome. But I know you know that." We both laughed."

How did you sleep?" I asked.

"I slept great. Better than I have been."

"Good, I'm glad to hear it. I can make some breakfast if you want?"

"I really want whatever you would cook but I promised to see my parents today and I definitely will have to go home and get ready."

"I understand."

"Definitely another time if you let me come over again... I hope. I really want to take you out again, Kelly. I like you a lot, as you know, and last night only increased that." I was blushing but not ready to say I was falling for him.

"Yes, I would go on another date with you."

"I'm glad to hear it." He kissed me on the forehead and then on the lips before getting up to get dressed. I put on my silk robe and quickly brushed my teeth. When I came back out of the bathroom Miguel was done. We walked to the door and he turned back and took me in his arms and kissed me for a minute and said, "I'm falling for you; hell, I think I might already love you." After that, he just left without saying another word. I closed the door and leaned against it, trying to gather my thoughts, but could only replay in my head what happened the night before.

A little later I was taking Brownie out for a walk when I heard someone call my name. I knew that voice. I turned in the direction and saw that I was right. After what Angela told me, I kind of figured this might happen. I didn't need further confusion to add my mind.

"Hey, Kyle."

"Hey, Kelly. Looking beautiful as always."

"Thanks, what brings you here?"

"Well, let's just say I hear not everything is good with you and your boy."

"Oh really? And who told you that?"

"I'm no snitch, so not telling." I respected that even though I already knew. I rolled my eyes.

"Well, it's none of your business, and I got to walk Brownie."

"I'll walk with you. Just hear me out."

"You're not going to stop, are you?" He shook his head. I sighed and I nodded. I started walking and he followed.

"Look, I know I did some things wrong but I would want you to give me another chance. I really like you, Kelly. The day when everything went left, I was going to ask you to be my woman. I still want you to be. I was attracted to you in the club and when you came to the gym and got to know you more, the attraction grew. You can't tell me you were not feeling the connection we had." I looked at him and then looked down and nodded.

"See? We should be together. We are good together, and seeing you with that guy... I wanted to beat his ass 'cause you were supposed to be with me. Also, I knew to officially back off but when I heard what happened at the firm, I just had to know if you were OK." The events of that day started playing in my head. I must have stopped walking because when I snapped out of my thoughts I saw that Kyle's face was filled with panic and concern. He had his arms around me and then I realized that I was in tears.

"I'm sorry that happened to you and everyone in that office." Then Miguel came to mind. I wiped my tears and thanked him. "I'm sorry for bringing it up in the first place."

"It's OK."

"I saw how that guy was looking for you when I was there, and it was genuine. I saw how you reacted when you saw him and I knew I needed to back off. Since he fucked up apparently, here I am."

"Look Kyle, yes he fucked up but that does not mean I'll give you another chance like that. You also ghosted me too for a while. Remember?"

"Yeah, and I apologized for that too. See, what happened was

I got arrested for beating a man's ass. I got bail but I did not want to face you and have you look at me differently.

"Why?"

"I'd rather not go into details." He was hiding things, again.

"Look, I don't hate you and don't have any ill feelings towards you, but I'm confused right now and I need to figure things out and make some decisions."

"What do you mean? You might get back with him or is there someone else?"

"Like you say, I do not want to go into details."

"Alright. Alright. Well, once you decide, hit me up." I just nodded. I arrived back at my apartment.

"I'm about to go back in."

"OK, and thank you for at least hearing me out." He stepped even closer to me with open arms. "Can I get a hug?" I leaned in and hugged him and as I started to get out of the hug and he kissed me.

"I just had to." Then he walked off.

I stood there for a second and walked towards my apartment. I realized at that moment that all the feelings that I had for him were gone. The kiss didn't make me feel anything anymore. At least I knew I did not have to be confused about three guys. Then Miguel and Zain came to mind. I knew I was now into Miguel (against my better judgment) but I still had love for Zain even though I rightfully disliked how he wanted to control my life.

Back inside my apartment, I received a message from Miguel.

Hey Sexy, hope you are having a good day. I know Monday will be the first day back in the office. I can either pick you up and we go together, or meet each other before going in so we can get through it together. Of course, you can say neither.

I responded.

Hey Handsome, I would say meet each other before going into the office just because I don't want office rumors to start. I appreciate it and I want to support you any way I can too.

He responded

You have already been showing support by being a strong woman. Also, you going on the date with me made me happy and the night was a bonus that I would love to repeat over and over. I would like for us to continue to go out on dates.

K: Awww Miguel, I would like to go out with you again. I also enjoyed the evening we had.

M: Glad to hear it. How about we plan to go to a movie after work on Tuesday or Wednesday.

K: Tuesday will be fine

We discussed Monday when we would meet up at the coffee shop near the office. I was grateful and felt more connected to him as we knew we need to get through it together.

The rest of the day was a self-care evening and binge watching on Netflix. The next day I woke up to a morning text from Miguel saying he was thinking of me. I smiled. Then there was the text from Lena, asking Angela and I to come over if we could that day. I responded with a yes. I got myself up, took a shower, and looked at myself in the mirror. I was toning up but could still see the rolls of flesh on my body and wondered how I attracted these guys. I hated it when I attacked myself even though there was nothing provoking it. I shook the thought out of my head and got ready.

22

CHAPTER 22

At Lena and Christian's condo, Lena wanted us to discuss plans for her wedding and enjoy a catch-up. We went over the potential timeline. Lena asked for both Angela and I to be bridesmaids, and we both accepted. Lena said her sister would be her maid of honor. After discussing plans, we switched to chatting about Angela and me. Angela and her guy were discussing their future and taking things slowly, but he was still treating her right. I told them what happened with Miguel and they were thrilled that he came into the picture. I also told them about what happened with Kyle and how I felt. They understood. We later drank and chilled for the rest of the evening. I was going back to the office that week, so before leaving the girls let me know they were one phone call away if needed. I really appreciated my friends.

The dreaded day arrived. It was time to go back to the office. I woke up and saw a text from Miguel letting me know what time he would be at the coffee shop. When I reached the coffee shop, Miguel had already put in our order.

"How are you feeling?" I asked him.

"I'm fine." He looked like he was forcing the smile but I could see through him. He was nervous and so was I.

"How about you?"

"I'm nervous but I know I'm not alone, and you are not alone either." I smiled, which seemed to help. We got our orders and walked to the building. We reached the entrance and paused and looked at each other and walked in. You can tell the office was cleaned from top to bottom. It was eerie. There was a sign saying "welcome back." I was happy that Miguel's office was only a couple of doors down from mine.

I reached my office and saw Rochelle at her desk. We hugged. I looked at Miguel and he gave me a nod and walked to his office. I went into mine and sat down. It felt so weird to be back. I zoned out for a minute until Rochelle brought me back to reality and I apologized. "I understand girl. I had to catch myself."

I was dreading the morning meeting that was arranged for the whole office. I knew it would be awkward talking about what happened that terrible day. A couple of hours later, it was time for the meeting. Rochelle had already headed to the meeting room. I left soon after and walked to Miguel's office. He was heading to the door. He pulled me inside his office, closed the door, took me in his arms and kissed me passionately. He released me from his kiss and looked into my eyes to see if I was OK. Without thinking, I put my hand to his face and caressed it, and he leaned his head into my hand. He then took my hand and kissed it. We backed away from each other and left his office to attend the meeting.

As I expected, they discussed that day and made a tribute to the people we lost. We lost five people that day, including Tim, the attorney who was close to a breakdown. Miguel was sitting across from me and we periodically made eye contact, though of course we played it off. After what seemed like forever, the meeting finally ended and we headed back to our offices.

Miguel was in front of me. When he reached his office he said, "You can come to my office whenever you want... if you need me." His eyes had the look of a man who would do anything to me and for me. I nodded and smile. I wanted to go into his arms but I knew better. I squeezed his arm gently and went to my office. A minute later Rochelle came in, closed the door and sat in front of me, staring at me.

"Yes, Rochelle?" I said. "You need something?"

"We cool right?"

I chuckled and nodded.

"Good... so what's going on with you and Miguel?" I did all I could to not react.

"What do you mean?"

"Oh, come on! I saw how he looked at you when you guys reached his office, and the way you squeezed his arm. That man had the look of love written all over his face."

"Rochelle...."

"We're cool, Kelly, and you know whatever we discuss has always stayed between us." She was not wrong. She proved that more than once. "Also, what about Zain?"

"Well, he and I broke up not too long after what happened because he wanted me to quit and I wouldn't do it."

"What the hell?! Yeah, I get it. I had hope for him too."

"So did I."

"So, what's the deal with you and Miguel?"

I knew Rochelle is good for remaining silent but I did not want to say anything still.

"Miguel and I became friends after what happened because he saved my life when he took the bullet. We are helping each other through the traumatic situation and we've just been making sure we're OK with everything now that we are back."

"Oh well, that's nice of you guys. But like I said before, Miguel likes you and I'm almost starting to think the 'like' has increased. I mean don't get me wrong, he is arrogant but nice too. You guys would make a cute couple but to go through the HR stuff... ugh." Rochelle reminded me of HR and knew that if Miguel and I kept going, we would have to notify them. She finally dropped it and went on with our day. Miguel and I texted throughout the rest of the day. We decided to go out for drinks after work.

We worked a little late and he met me in my office.

"You ready, Kelly?"

"Yes, just sending this last email."

I finished and grabbed my stuff and we went to a bar near his place so we would not be near the office.

"Damn, Kelly. Seeing you across the room in the meeting. I

wanted to come over and put your arms around you and kiss your lips and neck and just touch you. I wanted to put you on the table and fuck you right there." He was starting to turn me on. He leaned over and kissed my neck and I bit my bottom lip trying to contain myself. He noticed and said, "Do you know what you do to me when you bite your lip like that?" He paid the tab and took my hand and escorted me outside. "Kelly, I want and need you right now." He took me and kissed me as he did earlier and I returned his kisses. "Come back to my place, babe." I nodded.

We were only a block away so we walked to his place. On the way, he put his arms around my waist and held me tight. We reached his place and barely got through the door when we started making out. He started taking off my clothes and started taking off his. The kitchen island was not far and he put me on the island and took off my pants and underwear. He kissed my thighs and then kissed my pussy. He spread my pussy lips and started licking me and was getting wetter for him. He concentrated on my clit and did his work. He started to suck on it and let out a loud moan and grabbed his head. I wrapped my thick thighs around his head. I began pushing my pussy against his mouth. My breathing changed and feeling myself getting closer. "Right there! Don't....mmmm....don't stop." He didn't stop and the feeling took over and I leaned back came with a yelp.

He got up and he kissed me. I was getting off the counter and he helped me. I got on my knees and unbuckled his pants and let them drop, and pulled off his boxer briefs. I took his dick and licked his tip, and he moaned. I took him in my mouth and started licking and sucking. I was bobbing my head and he took his hand and grab my hair. "Fuck! Just like that Mamacita." I started massaging his balls while sucking. I continued and he grunted, then he came. I swallowed his cum. He looked at me with awe and took me in his arms and kissed me and then my neck and chest while rubbing me all over, then grabbing my ass and squeezing it.

Miguel took me to his bedroom. He put me on the bed and kissed me all over. He got on top and then he entered me and gasped. I grabbed onto his arms. He looked into my eyes as he started thrusting in and out of me. "FUCK! You feel so good... mmm...." He looked into my eyes as he was saying this and then kissed me with so much passion. I flipped him and got into the reverse cowgirl position and started riding him. I started moving my hips in a circle. He moaned loudly. He started meeting my thrust. "Shit baby the way your ass looks good slapping against my... Mmmmm."

He sat up, grabbed me by my neck and kissed me there. I turned my head towards him and he took my face and kissed me while I was still riding him. He then pulled me off and told me to get on my knees and then he started fucking me doggy style. He held my hips and started pumping his dick inside me. He gave me a few slaps on my ass. I yelled as he was going in deep.

"Does this feel good baby?"

"Yes! Fuck!" I met his thrust and we went crazy.

"I'm about to cum!!" I yelled.

"Damn babe, I am too."

We were both grunting and moaning and then we came. He held me so tight against him. Afterwards, we lay down. Miguel caressed my face and kissed me. I looked at the time — I didn't realize how late it was.

"I better go home; I don't want to go to work with the same clothes on."

We both laughed and got dressed, and he walked me to my car, which was next to his car. He kissed me while holding me tight.

By the time I reached my place, I had received two texts. One was from Miguel, asking me to let him know when I made it home. I responded. Then I looked at the other message. It was from Zain. I paused. He said he needed to talk to me about something important and he needed to see me that same night. Clearly that was not going to happen as I got in late. What else could he possibly want or need from me? I was not quitting my job. I replied, telling him that I got in late and that was getting ready for bed. A minute later he called me.

"Hey, Kelly." His deep voice gave me chills.

"What is going on?"

"I really need to see you."

"But I work in the morning."

"Please, babe." I had never heard this side of him. He sounded desperate. "Please see me even if it just for a few minutes. I'm already outside."

"Fine," I sighed. "Give me a minute." I put on a casual dress so I could easily take it off when I came back in.

I went outside and he was there. He got out and hugged me

before opening his car door for me to get in. He said he wanted to take me somewhere nearby.

"I did say I have to work in the morning."

"I know, it won't be long I promise." I was looking him over. He looked just as sexy as before, but I could see he was nervous, which was making me nervous. After about ten minutes we reached the dog park where we met outside of the class. He came around and opened my door. I got out.

"Why are we here?" I asked.

Zain took my hand and we walked towards the entrance and stopped. He continued to hold my hand and said,

"I want to first apologize for asking you to quit your job. I love you so much, and being without you hurts. You came into my life and made a huge impact on me. You are beautiful inside out and very intelligent. I miss you, Kelly, and I don't want to lose you. Seeing you with that guy... he doesn't deserve you. I want you in my life, baby, and I want to be the one to take care of you." Zain got on one knee and pulled out a small jewelry box. I saw a ring. "Will you marry me, Kelly?"

I was stunned. Hearing everything made me confused. My mind went all over the place. "Ummm, Kelly... babe?"

I looked at Zain with confusion. "I... I need to think."

He looked slightly disappointed. "I understand. Just please take the ring for now and think about it. I love you and want you to be my wife." He put the ring box in my hand and closed it. I was in such a daze I didn't even notice when we made it back to the car.

Neither of said anything on the ride back. When we reached

my apartment, Zain opened the door for me and I got out. "Please think about it. I'll be waiting by the phone to hear your answer. He gave me a hug and said goodnight. He leaned in and kissed me on my cheek and I looked into his eyes and he then kissed me while taking me into his arms and pressing me against his body. Tears formed as I realized I still love him. I grabbed his shirt and gripped it. We kissed for what seemed like an eternity. He broke the kiss and saw my tears and wiped them while caressing my face.

"I'd better go," I said. He nodded. I walked away but paused and looked back at him and he looked at me. He looked like he was about to walk toward me but I turned back around and left. Once inside, I leaned against the door and wept and slid down to the floor. Brownie jumped onto my lap. I just held him. I was completely confused.

At that moment I truly cared about two men, Miguel and Zain. I had a deep connection between both of them. I was mad at Zain for coming back into my life after pushing me away, but the love was still there. I got ready for bed and sat the ring on my nightstand before crying myself to sleep.

23

∞

CHAPTER 23

The next morning, I woke up tired but had to get up. I looked at my nightstand and saw the box. I realized it was not a dream. It really happened. I got myself together and saw good morning texts from Miguel and Zain.

Miguel:
Morning sexy. I can't wait to see you. Meet at the coffee shop again?
I responded-*yes*

Zain:
Morning gorgeous, I know I sprung the question out of nowhere after we had broken up but I want to be your husband. Take all the time you need to think. I'm here when you decide.

I went to the coffee shop and Miguel was there with my chai in hand. He looked around and then kissed me. I smiled.

"Is everything OK?" he asked. I nodded. "I'm a little tired."

"I'm sorry for keeping you out late. Did you want to postpone our date?"

"We can still go. I just need to get my day going."

We walked to the building and I reached my office. Miguel looked at me with a smile before entering his office. I pondered whether I should bring up what happened with Zain. I needed advice. I texted my girls to see if they could do lunch. I told them I needed advice about something. They both responded yes. I was somewhat relieved. I went on with my day as normally as I could. Miguel came into my office and closed the door. He pulled me off my seat and kissed me deeply and held me tight.

"I have been wanting to do that all morning."

I smiled and then there was a knock at the door. We quickly backed away from each other. Rochelle entered and was asking a question but then paused. She looked back and forth at us.

"Thanks for your assistance," said Miguel told her.

"You are welcome," she said.

Miguel left and closed the door behind him.

"Sooo, do you want to explain that?" Rochelle grinned.

"Explain what?"

"Come on. I know what I saw. You all both looked guilty."

I sighed.

"What I said was true. Miguel and I became friends but he came out and told me how he feels. He respected my relationship but, as you know, we broke up and Miguel knew about it. We've been out on a couple of dates and he is different outside of the office." My mind started to drift but Rochelle brought me back real quick.

"Gurl! See, I told you! You would not believe me when I said he liked you a lot. So, you must like him too?"

"I do. I surprised myself."

"Are you guys together yet?"

"No, we are not, but I also have a situation that just came up, as of last night."

"What situation?"

"Late last night Zain texted me saying he needed to see me. He didn't let up, so I finally agreed. To sum things up: he apologized and proposed to me."

"WHAT? Gurrrl! What did you say?"

"I told him I would think about it. I was just in shock."

"Do you want to marry him?"

"I... don't know... I mean the love is still there in spite of everything. But Miguel... he has been wonderful. I'm confused."

"Have you told Miguel?"

"No, not yet." I leaned back in my chair and sighed.

"Well, if Miguel is how you say he is outside of the office, then he will support you in whatever you decide." I nodded. We left it alone after and went back to work.

After an hour, it was time to meet up with my girls at the restaurant. After a quick talk about our day, they asked what was going on. I let them know about the evening with Miguel first, then I brought up Zain.

"He proposed last night, and I told him I would think about it. I'm confused. He kissed me and my feelings for him came rushing back in."

Angela and Lena looked at each other and then me with pity.

"We know that you were in love with Zain," Lena said, "but are you saying you have feelings for Miguel?" I zoned out thinking about Miguel and smiling. I looked at Lena and Angela and nodded. I looked down at my plate after barely taking a bite.

"Wow, talk about an entanglement. How about we make a list of pros and cons for both and go from there?" Angela suggested.

"What are some pros to Zain?" Lena asked.

"Zain is sexy with a deep voice. He has been there for me. He's great in bed. He always went out of his way to spoil me. He understands the struggles I've had and still have. We both love our dogs. He has shown he loves me."

"OK, now what are some of his cons?"

"He was a bit controlling when he asked me to quit my job. He is quick to anger. I question why he proposed to me now. He let me go when he could have stopped me. He...he hurt my heart." I felt tears coming on but I fought against them. Both Angela and Lena took my hands. "I'm sorry," I sniffed.

"There is nothing to apologize for," Angela said gently.

"Now to Miguel. What are his pros?"

"He's also sexy. Very intelligent. He fricking took a bullet for me, so he's proved he is willing to protect me. Once he opened up to me, he declared how much he cares for me. He's also great in bed and hearing him speak Spanish..." I bit my lip.

"Focus Kelly," said Lena. We chuckled.

I continued. "We have this bond due to what happened, and we understand and lean on each other. We comfort each other. He makes me laugh and challenges me."

"Now any cons?"

"He can be arrogant and nosey. We work in the same firm, which could potentially make things difficult. When he is mad, he shuts off."

"If we are going off of pure numbers then Miguel wins," Lena declared.

"We also know it's not that simple," Angela added. We all nodded.

"Things are still relatively new for me and Miguel. Should I tell him what happened with Zain?" They both were in my thoughts.

"I think you should. It will help determine how Miguel reacts to things," said Angela. Lena agreed.

"Also, it will let Miguel know this is not a game, and if he is serious about you guys then he needs to make it known. Plus, it shows open communication between the two of you," Lena said.

"You guys are right," I smiled. "I'll tell him. We have a date tonight, so I'll tell him then."

We finished our lunch and headed back to work. The rest of the day involved meetings. That evening, I changed clothes and met Miguel at my car to discuss our plans for the evening. We were going to the movies and then grabbing some food. We saw an action movie. Miguel had his arm around me the entire time. Kisses here and there. After the movie, we got a quick bite to eat. I was nervous about telling him what happened last night.

"Miguel?"

"Yes, sexy?" His smiled made it no easier. He noticed the look on my face and his happy expression faded to concern.

"Things between us have been great so far, and to see this different side of you outside of the office makes me like you more and more. I know we have a bond no one will understand. I like you a lot, and I mean a *lot*."

He smiled. "I really like you too, Kelly. I have feelings for you." He took my hand and kissed it. It sent a chill throughout my body.

"The reason I brought all this up is because.... something happened after I got home last night."

"What happened?"

"I received a text and then a call from my ex, Zain. The same one I just got out of a relationship with. He kept asking to see me, saying it was important. He was already parked outside my place. I eventually gave in and went outside. He took me to the place where everything started with us, and he proposed to me."

Miguel's face went from concerned to numb, then tense.

"What was your response...are you *engaged* to him?"

"No! I'm not engaged. No ring on my finger. If I were, I wouldn't be on this date with you right now." He calmed down and nodded.

"You know I'm still somewhat fresh out of the relationship and you know I cared about him. I was in shock when he did it. I was in a daze. I told him... I would think about it."

"Oh... do you want to marry him?"

"Honestly, I don't know if I want to. He hurt me and I'm confused. I thought the feelings I had for him were almost gone, if not completely. I care for you... a lot, and I'm developing feelings for you, Miguel." He looked dazed. I could not read him.

"Wow, he really couldn't let you go. I mean, I get it. I don't want to lose you but I also want you to be happy. I want to do all

I can to make you happy. If it's not me, and if he can do a better job than me, then I would have to let you go." I was shocked by his response. It was making me tear up and, at that moment, fall in love with him.

"I have not made a decision, Miguel. I don't know what to say. You impress me. I'm starting to wonder why you're even single."

"I have been hurt real bad before. I don't trust easily."

"I understand that too well."

"Kelly, what do you want to do?"

"Let me think about it. Is that, OK? I understand if you don't want to deal with me anymore."

"Babe, I'm not walking away from you. If anything, I will prove myself worthy of you. I'm not him. I will fight for you." I looked into his eyes and I knew his words were true.

We finished and left the restaurant. Miguel followed me home to make sure I got there safely. Then he walked me to my door.

"Babe, just know that I will not give up easily," he said. He then wrapped his arms around my waist and pulled me against his body and kissed me slowly but with urgency. I put my hand around the back of his neck and was returning his kisses. He pressed me against the door and I felt his body against mine. He was igniting me. My door was keyless so I moved my sensor until it connected and opened the door. I tossed my bag. Miguel took off his shirt and I pulled off mine. I took off my pants as he did the same.

By this time, we made it to my bedroom. We were kissing

and I backed up until I reached my bed and I fell back in my bed he pulled my underwear off and started rubbing my pussy. I let out a low moan. He then licked my pussy and started eating me out. I got so wet. He took a breath and looked around and said, "Hey Alexa, play 'Pussy is Mine' by Miguel." He looked at me as he said it. It started playing. He went back to eating me out. I felt his hand move up my body and he reached my bra and pulled one of my breasts out started rubbing my nipple. I pulled my other breast out and started rubbing it. I started moaning louder. I felt myself getting closer and closer. "FUCK!" I started shaking and he kept going and grabbing my hips. He didn't stop until I stopped moving, and that took me forever.

Miguel got up and took off his boxer briefs. "Alexa, play "Makin' Good Love" by Avant," he said. Then he got on top and spread my legs and slowly entered me. I grabbed his shoulders and we both grunted. He was slowly going in and out of me and he felt so good. He sucked on my nipple and looked up at me. I was massaging his head. While he was still inside me he sat up a little and pushed my knees to my chest and he continued to go in and out. He never stopped looking at me. He was going deep in me and I was moaning more loudly.

"You like this babe?"

"Yes, Miguel."

"Say it louder."

"YES, MIGUEL!"

"Say my name, sexy." He started to increase his speed. My mind was going into ecstasy. He was going faster and harder. He let my legs down and leaned in and kissed me so deeply. I was in love. I knew that now. I had my arms around him and I was about to cum.

"I'm about to cum!"

"Come for me, baby. I'm about to cum too." He went fast and hard. I felt myself coming and my nails dug into his back and I think I might have scratched his back. We both yelled out and held onto each other. We were trying to catch our breath but were kissing each other. He then caressed my face and smiled. I smiled back.

"Do you want to stay here?" I asked.

"Of course, I want to stay," he replied, "but I will have to leave early so I can get ready for work."

I nodded. He set his alarm and we fell asleep.

Hours later, I was woken up by my alarm. Miguel was gone but I saw a note. After adjusting my eyes, I read it.

Morning my beautiful sexy Kelly,

I did not want to wake you. You looked so peaceful. I know you will have to figure things out but I want you to know I will not stop trying until you tell me to stop. I can say so much more but I rather say it in person. See you in a few hours.

I smiled. Last night was just... wow. He gave it to me too good. As I was getting ready for work I couldn't help but relive the previous night. I was looking forward to work, to seeing him even though I had to act professionally. On my way to the office, I was listening to love songs and singing. At a stoplight a man in the car next to me was looking at me and I did not care. The light changed and I drove forward. But then a vehicle went through the light and was speeding towards me from my passenger side.

I blacked out.

24

CHAPTER 24

When I woke up, I was being pulled out of my car by a firefighter. I felt pain all over, and grunted.

"Good, you woke up. Don't worry you will be OK," the firefighter said. The EMT came and looked me over and asked me questions. My head was pounding. They indicated that I probably had a concussion. I was able to stand up and nothing seemed broken. I looked around and realized I was not far from the office. I saw my car. It looked in pretty bad shape. Definitely not safe to drive. They asked if I had anyone I could call, or they could take me to the hospital. The firefighter retrieved my bag. Thank goodness I had kept my phone inside it. It was still working.

As I was about to see who I could reach, I heard a voice. It was

Rochelle. She came rushing over. "Oh my god, are you alright? I saw your car and then I saw you!"

"I think I'm ok," I murmured. "My head is pounding so I think I need to go to the ER." The police on the scene told me my car would have to be towed. The other driver's car was also going to be towed. They were taken away in an ambulance. After everything was finished, I climbed into Rochelle's car. She called the office for me and let them know what had happened, and that she was taking me to the ER. I noticed she was texting too. The bruises all over my chest were kind of hurting. I think due to the seat belt. I thanked Rochelle for helping and she said no need. I closed my eyes trying to fight through the pain. My phone started buzzing. I couldn't be bothered to talk so I ignored it. A minute later it buzzed again. It was Miguel. I looked at Rochelle but she refused to look at me. I answered.

"Hello?"

"Kelly, are you ok? I heard what happened. Where are you? I can come to you."

"I'm OK. I'm just in a lot of pain all over. Rochelle is taking me to the ER. I'm guessing she told you." I looked back at her and she smiled with a "What?" expression.

"I can meet you at the ER," Miguel said.

"You don't have to do that. It would probably bring attention to us if you did."

"I know, but I don't care."

"Miguel, if we go to HR we need to do it together."

"I understand... OK, I'll just act like I'm meeting a potential client. That will work. See you there." He hung up before I could respond.

"I'm sorry but since I know you guys are kind of a thing, I thought you would want him to know."

I sighed.

"I get you. I just don't want to draw attention to us until we ready to talk to HR."

"You're right. I'm sorry."

"What's done is done."

We reached the ER and signed in. I sat in the chair just trying to get through the pain. After a little while I heard Rochelle say Miguel had arrived. I looked up and saw him walking quickly towards me, his face etched with worry.

"Hey," I said.

"Hey, babe." Miguel got on one knee in front of me and looked me over while he caressed my face. He looked into my eyes and saw how I was feeling. He kissed me on my forehead and sat beside me with his arm around me.

"Thanks, Rochelle, for everything," Miguel said.

"Of course!" Rochelle smiled. "I got her back."

"Thanks again, Rochelle. I really appreciate it," I said. She squeezed my hand.

"You don't have to stay if you don't want to, Rochelle. I will stay with her," said Miguel.

Rochelle said, "I will leave if Kelly wants me to."

I nodded. We said our goodbyes and continued to wait. Finally, I was able to see a doctor. Nothing was broken; I was just bruised with some scratches that required a couple of stitches. I did have a concussion. Not too long after, I was sent on my way. I called my insurance while Miguel was taking me home. There were still a couple of hours left before I could go to sleep. He stopped and got my prescriptions for me, then finally we reached home. He helped me get comfortable.

"Miguel, come here." I kissed him. He kissed me back.

"Thank you for helping me."

"Of course, you know I care about you. When I heard what a happened, I was just praying that you'd be ok. I don't want anything to happen to you. I couldn't think straight and just knew I needed to reach you and see you."

I caressed Miguel's face and he took my hand and kissed it.

"You better head back before they start to wonder where you are."

"Yeah, I guess you're right. I'll come back after work with some food. Also, if you need anything call me."

"OK," I said. He kissed me and left. I texted my close friends and told them what happened and let them know I was ok. They were praising Rochelle for helping (as they should) and for calling Miguel. I watched some TV until I was able to go to sleep. As soon as I could I did.

A little while later, I was woken by a knock at the door and Brownie barking. I got up slowly and looked to see who it was. Miguel. I opened the door and I smelled tacos. He knew I loved tacos. He walked in and kissed me and asked how I was feeling. I still felt crappy but was glad I was able to sleep. He bought the tacos from a food truck. Those are the best ones. He set everything up and we ate and watched a movie.

"You did not have to do this but I appreciate it, and thank you," I said.

"No thanks needed, sexy. You helped me through my recovery.

And what makes you think I wouldn't do the same for you?" I smiled and took him by his dress shirt and kissed him. We made out for a little bit and then he broke off. "Sorry, I just want to make sure I don't hurt you." I grabbed him again and kissed him passionately.

"Hey, I went by my place and grabbed some things. If you like I can stay here with you for a couple of days?"

"OK," I smiled.

"OK, good. Let me run out to my car and get my bag." He got up and went to his car. I looked at my phone and saw a text from Zain.

Hey Gorgeous. I just wanted to check in and see how you were doing, and if you had thought about the proposal.

I replied:

I'm ok and yes; I have thought about it and I will let you know my answer this weekend.

He responded with an "OK." I did not want to tell Zain what happened because I knew that if I did he would show up. Even if I told him Miguel was here. I was thinking about Zain up until Miguel came back. I knew I needed to make a decision by the weekend. The rest of the evening was calm. Miguel took care of me and we watched TV. I emailed my office to notify them that I was off for the rest of the week. Miguel helped me to bed after taking a shower. I started to doze off while he sat in bed beside me, working on his laptop. He kissed me goodnight and I felt at peace.

I woke up the next morning feeling stiff. I looked over and I was the only one in bed. It was 10 am, so Miguel must have gone to the office. I replied to a few texts from people checking on me. Then I saw a text from Miguel:

Morning sleepyhead,

I know you will probably be stiff so I made sure to leave your meds on the counter, and a plate of food in the fridge. I will check on you late. If you need anything let me know. Also, I'm glad you are letting me stay with you for a couple of days to make sure you are ok.

He put a smile on my face. I replied:

Morning Handsome. I'm feeling a little stiff, I appreciate what you are doing for me, and thank you.

After eating I did some work on my laptop and made some work calls. Rochelle and Miguel both messaged me, telling me to stop working. They were right. I took Brownie outside for a walk in the mini dog park in the complex, then I rested afterwards. Eventually. I knocked out. I woke up to a knock on the door. I opened it and it was my girls. They came to check on me and were glad to see I was not badly hurt. We talked for a while. I mentioned that Miguel was taking care of me and that he knew about the proposal. Lena and Angela both said he gave a great response to it. They then asked if I had made a decision. I told them I was still thinking about it but I was leaning toward the answer. We hung out until Miguel came back and they wanted us to have some alone time. After they left, Miguel made dinner and we talked about our day. The rest of the evening was good, and I fell asleep in his arms.

The next day I woke up with Miguel already gone. He had left another morning message. I thought about my decision over Zain's proposal. I knew I cared about both men and love them both. I thought about Zain and Miguel in terms of personalities, sex and potential future. After evaluating everything I finally made my decision.

First things first: I called Kyle.

"Hey, Kyle."

"Hey, beautiful," he responded. "How are you?"

"I'm ok, how are you?"

"Good, and glad you called. I take it you figured things out?"

"Yes, I have. We had a great connection together but after everything that happened... I think we're better off as friends. I don't hate you but I feel we are better off that way."

"OK.... well, I guess there's nothing left to be said. I'll see you around."

"I'm sorry."

"It's cool. I got to go. Thanks for letting me know." After that, he hung up.

I texted Zain to come over. A few minutes later he replied that he would be on his way soon. I tried to get myself together as nice as I could while still being in some pain. Half an hour later I heard a knock. I opened the door and there was Zain, looking fine and with flowers. He smiled until he saw the stitches and the bruise on the side of my forehead.

"What the hell happened to you?" He caressed my face. I closed the door and went to the couch. He put the flowers on the coffee table.

"I was in a car accident but I'm OK. Just had a concussion, bruises and scratches."

"When did this happened?"

"On Wednesday but I'm OK. I can't say that about my car. It is most likely totaled. An idiot ran a light and hit me." He shook his head and grew angry.

"Why didn't you call me?"

"I was in so much pain. My assistant actually showed up at the accident, since it was close to the office, and picked me up. Also, the fact we broke up." Zain looked down for a second.

"She was cool when I met her so I can believe it. I'm happy you're OK."

"Thanks. I called you because I thought about the proposal and I have made a decision."

"Great. And before you give me the answer I just want to say I love you and even though we broke up, I could never get you off my mind. I was missing you. I want a future with you and to have kids."

"That's very sweet. I thought about it. I do love you and you have been there for me. I also thought about the fact that you were making me choose who I am and what I worked so hard for. You get angry quickly but also can be really sweet. You also asked me to marry you when you realized I could move on. You let me leave that day when we could have never broken up. I love you but my answer is no. I'm sorry." He looked down and did not say anything. He then nodded his head. I went to my bedroom and fetched his ring and handed it to him. Zain took the box and then looked at it. I could see the hurt in his eyes.

"OK, I get it. How about we just get back together as boyfriend and girlfriend and we work on us?"

"Zain, I think it's best to leave things here. It is best if we don't get back together because it would be for the wrong reasons. I have done the back and forth with guys before and I don't want to do that. If we are meant to be then we will find our way back to each other."

"I know it is because of that guy. You are supposed to be with me. You are not like any other woman I have met. You deserve everything. Please reconsider."

"Please don't make it harder than it already is."

"Fine! I will go." Zain got up and headed to the door but then turned and looked at me. "Just know I will always love you and I hope you will be happy." He left. I sat there for a second and tears fell down my face. I loved him but I knew it would not work out in the long run. I got myself together. I texted my close friends. They all supported my decision. I then took a nap until I heard knocking on my door. It was Miguel.

"Hey sexy," he said. He took me in his arms and kissed me. How are you feeling?"

"I'm still in pain but better than I was."

"Good! If you want me to go home, I can. If you want me to stay, I can do that too."

"Yeah, you can stay if you want to."

"Great! I was hoping you would say that. We can order some food and relax. I can give you a massage."

"Mmmmm, that does sound great." I put my arms around his

shoulders and kissed him for a minute. "Thanks again for taking care of me."

"You are welcome, sexy. You deserve it."

We were relaxing on the couch and he talked about what was going on at the office. Then he asked me about my day.

"It was good and I have something to tell you."

He tensed up.

"OK, what's up?"

My ex came by because I asked him to come. The reason why is because I made a decision about the proposal and gave him my answer.

Miguel cleared his throat. "What was your answer?"

"I told him no, I can't marry him."

Miguel let out a sigh of relief and smiled.

"I'm not going to hide how happy I am that you turned him down." For a minute he made a look as if deep in thought, then he looked at me.

"Kelly?" He took my hands and held them.

"Yes, Miguel?"

"Is there anyone else?"

"No, not at this time."

"Well, since there is no one else, I want you to know I have fallen in love with you. I know we are not officially together but I want you to know where I stand."

"Miguel, I'm falling in love with you too." A big smile spread across his face and he kissed me with urgency. He gathered me in his arms and hugged me tightly. I think he forgot I was still in pain. I let out a small yelp.

"I'm so sorry mi amor. I didn't mean to hurt you."

"I know, I know," I chuckled.

"I would love it if you were to become my girlfriend. But before you make that decision, I want to make sure it is something you really want. So, how about this weekend we spend time together and maybe if you decide, you can let me know if you want to be my woman and me be your man this Sunday evening. Also, if we do move forward together, we can tell HR on Monday."

I paused and just looked at him. There was no reason to deny him.

"OK, let's do it."

25

CHAPTER 25

Miguel and I spent the rest of the evening cuddling and watching TV. He even gave me a massage, which knocked me out for the night. The next morning I was still healing but improving. Miguel was already up. I was not a morning person like him.

"Morning babe," he said while making pancakes in the kitchen.

"Morning my lover," I said with a chuckle. He laughed and gave me a gentle hug and asked how I was feeling. I let him know I was improving. I helped him make breakfast as much as he allowed me anyway. After breakfast, we got ready and took Brownie for a walk. Miguel made sure to hold me close to him with his arm around my waist. He was sneaking kisses on my neck and when I look at him, he kissed me on my forehead and then my lips. After our walk, he took me to get a manicure and pedicure, and then shopping. We went back and forth about him buying stuff for me. He would not hear of me buying anything myself. He said he wanted to spoil me. After the shopping we went out for dinner and laughed and talked. He made me feel at ease but, in the back of my mind, I was still concerned about our relationship. I think I was scared of things going wrong.

When we returned to my place, we got comfortable and listened to music and talked. Luther Vandross and Beyonce's song "Closer I Get to You" came on. As I began swaying to the music, Miguel stood up and held his hand out to me. I gave him my hand. He pulled me up and into his arms and held me close to his body. We slow danced with our fingers intertwined, and he put my hand to his lips and kissed it while looking into my eyes. He started singing along to the song. I had realized that he could not sing but loved how he tried to anyway. I was trying to holding in my laughter. He noticed and smiled and then we both started giggling. He then caressed my face and kissed me deeply and I returned his kiss. While continuing to kiss, we sat back down on the couch and made out for a while. He was gently stroking my body all over then said, "We should head to bed." He rose back up, pulled me up and led me to the bedroom.

He took off my top and then my bra. He took each one of my breasts into his mouth and lightly sucked on my nipples. "I know you are still healing so I don't want to cause any pain but I want you to feel good." He had me sit down on the bed and pulled my pants and underwear off. He took off his shirt. He then leaned over me and kissed me on my lips then my neck and then continued down and kissed both of my inner thighs. He kissed the outer lips of my pussy, which caused me to let out a moan and bite my lower lip. He gave me a sexy grin. He continued to make eye contact with me and licked my pussy and then sucked on my clit. My breathing became ragged and it felt so good. He took a breath and stuck a couple of fingers in my pussy and put his thumb on my clit and started rubbing. He was getting me closer and closer. He went back to eating me out and I came hard. I tried to subdue my yell by covering my mouth. He got up with a smile on his face. We got into bed and fell asleep in each other arms.

The next day I woke up and saw Miguel was still asleep. I just stared at his sexy ass for a minute and smiled while watching him sleep so peacefully. As happy as I was with him I could not help but have worries about our potential relationship. He had proven over and over that he cared. Even when we had sex, he was making love to me. I also thought about his cockiness and how that got on my nerves but I understood why he acted like that at work. I would never believe a man this fine would want someone like me. As much as I had been working on my confidence, the doubts lingered. I was also worried about the firm. One of us would have to switch departments or go to a different firm altogether. I mean, he was a junior partner and I was on that track.

Feeling better, I went to the bathroom and noticed that many of my stitches had dissolved. I was starting to feel like myself again. I turned on the shower. As I was about to get in, Miguel came into the bathroom and looked at me with a grin on his face.

"Morning, mi amor." I smiled at him back and he came up

to me and kissed me. I got in the shower and he followed. I got my scrubber and started to lather myself where I could without messing with my stitches. Miguel then took my scrubber and rubbed my back for me. I rinsed off and then I did the same for him. I touched his body as he touched mine. I got to his dick and cleaned it and massaged it. He let out a moan and I kissed him. I turned off the water. He pulled me closer and we started making out. I continued going up and down with my hand before massaging his balls. I had a built-in seat in my shower, so I backed up and sat down and took his dick in my mouth and started sucking and letting my tongue roam on his cock. He put his hand on my head and said, "Maldita sea nena, eso se siente demasiado bien (Damn babe, it feels too good). He let out a moan and I got faster and he came. He lifted me up and kissed me deeply. He sat down and turned me around so I was facing away from him. He the sat me down on his lap and had me leaning against him. He spread my legs open and started massaging my pussy and rubbing my nipple. I let out a small moan and looked at him. He looked into my eyes and then up and down my body.

"You are so fucking beautiful." He kissed me. I moved his fingers up and down my lips. He put a finger in and went in and out. I let out a gasp. He kissed me again, and kissed my neck. He moved back up to my clit and starting rubbing more and I felt myself get closer. I started moaning more and started moving my hips against his hand. "That's its babe, cum for me. Cum on my hand." I climaxed and let out a loud grunt.

"Kiss me, Miguel!"

He did just that while still rubbing me. When I came back

down from my orgasm, we cleaned ourselves again and got out of the shower.

We decided to go out for breakfast at an outdoor café. We were enjoying ourselves until I saw Kyle walking up to me. *Fuck, can I stop running into him?*

"Hey, Kelly."

"Hey, Kyle. How are you?"

"I'm alright and you?" His irritation grew when he saw Miguel.

"I'm good. Thanks for asking." He nodded and looked back at Miguel. I knew I better introduce otherwise it would be more awkward.

"Miguel meet Kyle; Kyle meet Miguel." They both said hi and nodded at each other. Miguel looked like he was starting to put two and two together.

"So, are you her boyfriend?" Kyle asked.

"Well, not yet but I'm hoping she will let me be soon," said Miguel with a smile. He then took my hand and kissed it. I glanced at Kyle and saw his nostrils flare but he kept a straight face. Then I looked back at Miguel who had read the situation and was smiling. He was enjoying this.

"I better go. Nice meeting you, man. You better take care of her," Kyle said. He looked at me and nodded and walked away. "He was the other guy that had your attention for a while?" said Miguel.

I nodded. "I'm honestly glad they both messed up. Otherwise, I would not have been able to be with you like I am today." He leaned over and kissed me. His kiss felt so sweet. I looked at him and caressed his face as he smiled. I ran my finger over his dimple. He turned his head and kissed my hand. A tingling sensation ran through my body.

"I noticed how much you enjoyed making him mad."

Miguel laughed.

"Yeah, of course. You know me. His loss is my win, and the fact he realized he lost someone who's priceless."

"Oh, aren't you feeling yourself. That was a smooth line."

"No, I'm feeling you and it's the truth." He said that with a straight face. It shut me up.

"OK, today is Sunday and I know we decided to talk about us. Do you want to talk about it now," he said. I look at him and my mind was made up.

"Yes, we can." He let out a sigh and sat up straight.

"Kelly, you know I have fallen in love with you. When I first heard about you at the office, I heard you were a pretty good attorney. Of course, I'm better," he said with a wink. I rolled my eyes and laughed. "I looked you up and noticed that you were attractive but I also viewed you as my competition. When we got assigned together I was going to take the time to learn more about you so I could know how to compete with you. Instead, I started to really like you. I was trying to fight it but obviously, I couldn't. I would love it if you'd become my girlfriend Kelly. Will you have me?"

I looked into his eyes and said, "Miguel, you are very attractive. I noticed that when I first met you. I also noticed how cocky you were right off, and could not stand you. You drove me nuts with your interrogation. I found myself wondering why it ended abruptly and shook the thought that you might like me. Even when someone told me you liked me I was denying everything. I'm not saying their name." He closed his eyes and shook his head. I knew, he knew who told me. "I could no longer ignore what was happening between us, and when.... when you took that bullet for me, I started to see a different side to you and we developed a bond because of it. I could not fight it. I have fallen for you. So, my answer is.........yes.

After I responded, Miguel got up and pulled me out of my seat and into his arms, and kissed me deeply. When we finally broke from our kiss, we both smiled at each other and didn't say a word.

26

CHAPTER 26

We finished up our meal and went back to my apartment. We barely made it through the door and we were making out.

"Mi armor," Miguel said, "I'm happy you said yes and I want to show you how much." He took me to the bedroom and took off my clothes, then his. He laid me down and started kissing me all over my body. He turned me on my stomach and gave me a massage, rubbing his hands all over my body. I let out a moan as he hit the areas, I needed the most attention in. I was starting to feel more relaxed and I let a few moans. "Baby, you keep making noises like that...getting me turned on more than I already am."

"I'm sorry love, you just massaging all the right areas."

"O really?" Then I felt his mouth on my neck as he gave me kisses. His kisses went on down my back and then kissed my ass, followed by a slap on my ass. "Sorry, I just had to," he said. I chuckled. He continued massaging me. It felt so good, I was starting to fall asleep. That was until he turned me around on my back. He kissed me and then my neck. He started massaging my left breast with one hand then the right one with his other hand. He went back and forth sucking on each nipple. He then took one hand and started massaging my pussy. He leaned he up and kissed me. He was getting my juices flowing. He then spread my pussy lips and gave it a long lick. I squirmed under his tongue. He flicked his tongue on my clit. I grabbed his hair and pushed my hips forward. He started licking my pussy like crazy. I felt myself getting closer, but then he stopped and got up.

Miguel maneuvered until he was on top of me. "I want to be inside you," he said. "I'll be gentle 'cause I don't want to hurt you. I know you're still healing." I nodded. He entered me slowly. I felt every inch filling me up. I looked at him and told him to kiss me. He leaned down and kissed my lips, then his tongue found mine. We were making out and letting our tongues dance while he started thrusting in and out of me. He switched to my kissing my neck and lightly sucking on it. He leaned up and gave me long deep strokes. Both of us grunted and looked deep into each other eyes. "Fuck baby, I love you," he said, and kissed me passionately.

"I love you too," I said.

Miguel smiled and said, "I'll go a little faster and a little harder. Let me know if it is too much baby, OK?" I nodded. He started to increase speed and held my hips. We were both in ecstasy. I was moving my hips a little bit to meet his thrust. We started to get louder. We reached a point we didn't care about anything. I leaned up towards him and he wrapped his arms around me and put his hand on my ass. We were making out while he was still pounding me. We were both making noises and then we climaxed and yelled out while coming together. I was shaking. He held me tight and I felt his dick throbbing while I know he was feeling my pussy do the same. We calmed down and lay in each other arms and talked.

"So about work tomorrow...." I said.

"Yeah, I know we've got to talk about it. How do you want to go about this?"

"Ummm, good question." We both laughed. "We can go by the HR department in the late afternoon towards the end of the day."

"Yeah, that can work."

"I'm just nervous they would want to separate us or ask one of us to quit."

"No matter what happens, we will get through it together." He kissed me.."Plus, I also have a background in litigation so I can always switch over."

"You got junior partner being in this department though. It will slow you down for senior."

"You're worth it baby, and you've never seen me in action for litigation. I'm a beast."

I chuckled and shook my head. "OK, it's settled. I will be in late. I have a doctor's appointment in the morning."

"Aww babe you should have told me, I would have taken time off to go with you."

"That would make things real obvious at work," I laughed.

"True. I know you're waiting on the settlement for your car.

I can at least drop you off at the appointment, and maybe I can sneak away to get you. It's better than getting a Lyft."

"What would I do without you, love?"

"I have no idea." We laughed. We spent the rest of the day lounging around. He went home to get ready for the week but planned to get me in the morning. I got myself together for the week and went to bed early.

I woke up the next morning feeling refreshed. I got ready. Miguel barely arrived on time. I had to rush out and he apologized and put on a sad face. I forgave him when there was coffee waiting for me. He dropped me off at the doctor's office and left. The appointment went fine, the doctor said I was healing up nicely. I didn't want to pull Miguel from the office so when I was done I got a Lyft. As I approached my office, Rochelle was waiting for me.

"Hey, boss, glad to see you back!" She hugged me and I gave her one back.

"I wanted to say thanks again for being there for me. I owe you so let me know how I can repay you."

"Oh gurl, you don't have to do anything."

"Nope, I will figure it out on my own then." We laughed and went into my office. Rochelle closed the door, sat in front of me and just stared. I read her face. I knew she wanted updates about me and Miguel.

"What's on your mind, Rochelle?"

"Oh, you already know. How are things between you and Miguel? The way that boy came to you at the hospital... he is in love."

I looked at her a second. She gave me a knowing look.

"OK, OK. We're great actually. We made it official between us and will be talking to HR later today."

"I knew it! He came in today looking real happy. He had a stupid grin on his face." Rochelle leaned in and said, "You must have put it on him good."

I shook my head with a smile and said, "No comment."

"Uh huh." We laughed for a good minute and carried on with our work. I did get a short speech from Miguel as to why I didn't let him come get me, but we settled it with kisses in his office.

Later on, Miguel appeared at my door. I knew it was time. We went to the next floor where the manager was expecting us. There was an older woman who looked like she was unhappy with her life. We told her we wanted to date each other and notify them in accordance with the rules. We stated we would not let our relationship interfere with our job. The manager made it clear they didn't care what we said but, as per protocol, one of us had to switch departments. Miguel let them know he could move. It was settled after that. We were officially allowed to be together without issue.

Miguel was planning to move over to the other side tomorrow. I was working late while he packed up his stuff. We were pretty much by ourselves at the office. I completed my work and went to his office. He was just about finished. He saw me and came to me with a kiss before closing the door. I smiled at him, knowing what that meant.

"Babe, we can't! What if someone catches us."

"They won't baby, they all left for the day." He took me in his arms and started making out with me. I could not resist him. He pulled me to his desk and lay me down on it. He unbuttoned and unzipped my dress pants, pulling them off while I unbuckled his pants and let them drop. We lifted my shirt just above my chest and started sucking on my nipples. I fought the urge to moan in case someone heard us. I pulled his boxer briefs down and he peeled off my underwear, then started eating my pussy wildly. Licking and sucking. I grabbed his head as it was sending me over the edge. I think I pushed his head too much because at one point he started tapping my thigh. I let go. He was breathing heavily.

"I'm sorry," I whispered.

"It's OK, mami, I just don't want to die here. I rather die in one of our places."

We chuckled. Miguel then put his dick inside slow and deep. I put my arms around his neck. He caressed my face and we started making out as he pounded me. I heard him mumble "fuck" and something else in Spanish. It started feeling too good. I reclined all the way until my back was on the desk. He grabbed my hips and continued to go fast and hard. We went at it with so much passion, and when we finally came he held onto my hips as he was cumming inside me, pressing hard against me. We caught our breath, got dressed and left the office holding hands.

Six months later....

Lena was still planning her wedding six months away. Angela and I were doing whatever we could to help. She was planning an extravagant ceremony. A destination wedding in Jamaica. The invitations just went out. Angela and I were trying to figure out her bachelorette party. We knew we wanted to do it right.

Miguel and I were going strong as ever. He was thriving in his department and I made junior partner. It seemed we could not get enough of each other. Always making love in so many different places. Our six-month anniversary was coming up. Miguel said he wanted to plan something special but would not tell me what. When it got closer to the day, he told me we were going to Hawaii for our anniversary. I had never been there; I was so excited. I went shopping for the trip and brought my girls with me. They helped me pick outfits and we had fun. I had my hair done in goddess locs and got myself looking the best I could for this vacation. I picked my swimsuits and showed Miguel. All he did was lick his lips and said, "Mmmm, can't wait to have you in my arms walking on the beach." He made me feel beautiful.

When the day came, we had to catch an early flight. Miguel had bought first-class tickets for both outbound and connecting flights. When we landed in Maui, he picked up the SUV rental and drove us to our hotel. It was beautiful. We dropped off our bags in the suite and started our vacation. On the first day we went to the beach and joined a tour the next day. On the third night, Miguel told me he made some dinner plans for our anniversary. I dressed up cute and wore makeup and let my locs flow. We headed to dinner and saw we had a private table on the beach. The food was delicious. I noticed that Miguel was acting weird while the dessert was coming.

All of sudden, I heard someone singing, and then a group appeared and sang, *With You* by Tony Terry. That was one of my favorite songs. He must have noticed. I was in shock. The singers were killing it. I turned to look at Miguel and the next thing I see is him bending down in front of me on one knee and saying, "Kelly, just like this song says, when I'm with you what I feel is real. You came into my life as a rival but quickly became my everything. You made me so happy and I will try my hardest to do the same for you. I love you so much.... what I want to know is if you will please do me the honor and marry me so I can give you the world, baby." He opened the ring box and I saw a big rock. I was in pure shock and tears started streaming down. I was speechless but then he snaps me out of it when he said, "Mi amor?"

I shook myself out of it and looked at him and immediately said, "YES! YES! YES!" He put the ring on my finger and it fit. He got up and put his hand to my face, wrapped his arm around me, and kissed me with so much passion. I kissed him with the same intensity. When we finally broke from kissing, tears were still coming and he was wiping them away and looking into my eyes. "You made me so happy. I can't wait for you to be my wife." The group applauded and congratulated us.

"I can't wait for you to be my husband. Wait, how did you know my ring size?"

Miguel cleared his throat.

"I measured your finger while you were sleeping one day." We laughed and kissed again. We did not need any dessert. The group played another favorite, *Fortunate* by Maxwell. We slow danced and kissed throughout the song. We applauded them. After the celebrations we went back to our room. As soon as the door closed, we started kissing and Miguel went to my neck, kissing and licking while he unzipped my dress and let it drop. I unbutton his shirt and pulled it off as fast as I could. He took off my bra and I unbuckled his pants and pulled them down. He lay me on my back at the edge of the bed and pulled off my underwear. Pushing my nipples close together, he flicked his tongue on both of them at the same time. It was turning me on so much. I arched my back for him. He started sucking on each one. He took one hand and rubbed my pussy and teased my clit. I yelled out, "Fuck, that feels so good." He went further and stuck a couple of fingers in my pussy. While fingering me he went down and started licking my clit. He was looking at my sex face and was so turned on.

I wanted Miguel to feel good. I told him to stop and he said, "What's wrong, baby? Did I do something?" No, I told him with a smirk on my face. Then I got up and sat him down and took his dick in my hand and stroked it up and down. He moaned and looked at me. I continued to stroke while I massaged his balls and then sucked on each one. He was squirming and I loved it. I then put his dick in my mouth. He started licking and sucking as I bobbed up and down on his dick. He leaned back a little bit and he was massaging my head then grabbed my hair. He yelled out. He then pulled me off his dick and put me back on the bed. He looked like he wanted to do everything to me. He had my ass off the edge of the bed and put my legs up and against him, then put a pillow under me. Slowly but deeply he entered me. He was going slow and steady, in and out, like he wanted me to feel every inch of him. He started in my eyes and all I saw was love. He stared into my eyes and all I saw was love. "I am all yours and you are all mine.

"Yes, Miguel. All yours."

"That's right, mi amor. You're going to be my wife. I will make love to you whenever we want.

"YES! Papi."

"SHIT. Call me Papi again."

"Papi! You're my Papi." He started going faster and harder, moving his hips and making sure he gave me long strokes. We both were breathing hard. I was matching his thrust and we were loud but did not give a damn. He was pounding my pussy while kissing my leg and rubbing my clit.

"Mmmmm, I'm so close. I'm about to cum, Papi!"

"Yes, Mami, cum on your dick. I'm about to come too... shit!" We were going crazy, the bed was moving a lot and we were cumming together. He pressed his hip hard against me, making sure he released every bit of him in me. We were coming off our high and he leaned in and kissed me deeply. He grabbed my hand. My pussy was still throbbing and so was his dick. I could still feel it pulsing. Afterward, we cleaned ourselves up and got in bed, and lay in each other arms.

"How does it feel to be the future Mrs. Rodriguez?"

I chuckled.

"Well, it will be Mrs. Turner-Rodriguez but it feels really good." Then I kissed him. He nodded and smiled in agreement. We lay there just enjoying the silence, except for the sound of the waves from the ocean. Miguel fell asleep first. I just looked at him. The fact that I was happy was surreal. I had a good man who I would get to spend the rest of my life with. He was so handsome, smart, caring and funny. And he loved me.

I started to think about everything and how we got here. We went through a lot. I was also happy with myself. I was able to continue to build my confidence and value my worth. I was able to overcome my internal struggles to get here. I'm a beautiful woman who deserves happiness and a man who loves me. Yes, I'm a plus-size woman and someone who is feeling myself and deserves all. Yes, I might have my moments but just had to throw those negative thoughts out of my mind and move on to bigger and better things.

SHIT! I had to bring him to my family. This was going to be interesting. Could he survive them?

ABOUT THE AUTHOR

Naomi Hines was born and raised on the south side of Chicago. As a plus size African-American woman, she did not see a lot of representation of plus size women in romance novels. Also, as an introvert with an active imagination and dating life experience wanted to contribute to the genre. When not writing and/or dating, spends time with the important people in her life and go on adventures as a love of traveling runs deep.

www.ingramcontent.com/pod-product-compliance
Lightning Source LLC
Chambersburg PA
CBHW071526120726
47907CB00013B/1090